THE WISH TO KILL

THE WISH TO KILL

Janet Hannah

Published in the United States by

Soho Press, Inc.
853 Broadway
New York, N.Y. 10003

Library of Congress Cataloging-in-Publication Data

Hannah, Janet, 1939–/
     The wish to kill/Janet Hannah.
        p. cm.
        ISBN 1-56947-177-0 (alk. paper)
        I. Title.
     PS3558.A47624W57   1999
     813'.54—dc21   99-26918
                               CIP

10   9   8   7   6   5   4   3   2   1

ACKNOWLEDGMENT

I would like to acknowledge Gaby Levy and the other dedicated professionals at Jerusalem Productions for their invaluable help in preparing the manuscript.

CHAPTER 1

"Go to hell!" Alex said. He was alone in the room and he said it under his breath, in Hungarian. Even so, the word *hell* had barely passed his lips when a violent explosion echoed down the corridor in answer to his command.

After an instant of stunned disbelief, he jumped out of his chair and ran past the dark, deserted laboratories toward the source of the noise. Tendrils of foul-smelling smoke drifted out of the doorway of the one lighted lab. It belonged to Ilan Falk, the man he had just been thinking about. Professors Shiloh and Blum, whose offices were nearby, were already at the door.

David Shiloh took a deep breath and went in first. Yekeziel Blum was close behind, waving his arms wildly to clear the air in front of his face. Alex followed slowly, hoping that whoever had turned on the light was somewhere else. Otherwise, there was no appealing explanation for the silence.

If Ilan Falk was somewhere else, it was only in spirit. His body was lying on its back with its feet toward the door. They inadvertently hesitated as his head came into view, and they realized that his face had taken the full force of the explosion.

Alex knelt beside the body and picked up one wrist. Near the floor, the smell of gas was strong enough to be notice-able in spite of all the competing odors. It felt strange to be checking for vital signs without a confusing din in the back-ground, but in this case it wouldn't have mattered.

"There's no pulse," he said.

Yekeziel said, "Thank god!"

David Shiloh found that he had been holding his breath. He exhaled in relief.

The lab was surprisingly intact for the scene of a fatal explosion. The damage was confined to the area around the body, and was limited to some smashed bottles whose con-tents mingled on the bench top and dripped onto the floor, and a few smoldering plastic objects. A cardboard carton and its polystyrene packing material, blazing merrily, seemed to be responsible for most of the smoke. David Shiloh quickly doused it.

Flame leaped in the air above, but not touching, a bunsen burner on the bench in front of where the body lay. This was so clearly a case in which the fire had been carried to the burner on a trail of gas, rather than originating at the burner's surface, that no one bothered to mention it. Alex shut off the gas supply, then went to open the windows. In the meantime, tall, silver-haired David Shiloh tried ineffec-tually to clear shards of broken glass from around the body, making an effort not to look at the face. Round, balding Yekeziel Blum dialed 101, the Red Star of David, for an ambulance.

"He lit a cigar," David told them as he stood up. The tin box the cigar had come from was on the floor near Ilan's hand, and David could detect a trace of its pungent odor mingled with the other smells. "He never could give up the habit, even though the doctors told him it was dangerous for his health." There was a short silence. "I didn't intend to be funny," he muttered.

David and Alex followed Yekeziel to the telephone, because it was at the side of the lab opposite to where Ilan lay—and his body was out of sight from there.

"An ambulance is on its way," Yekeziel said as he replaced the receiver. "Alex, did you open all the windows? How could he not have smelled the gas? And what kind of a harebrained idea was it to light a cigar at the workbench? Even beginning students know better than to smoke in the labs!"

There were six laboratories on the fourth floor of the biology building at the University of Jerusalem. They were large rooms that looked like the workshops they were, with fluorescent lights suspended on chains from high ceilings and exposed, color-coded pipes. White plastic-surfaced workbenches lined both walls and formed a peninsula down the center. A small alcove, just large enough for a desk and bookshelf or file cabinet, opened off one of the side walls at the end farthest from the doors. Rows of shelves were crowded with brown glass jars that held chemicals and clear glass bottles that held prepared solutions.

Although it was late, all three felt obliged to stay until the ambulance came. It would have been unfair for one of them to slip away and leave the others to stand the vigil.

Yekeziel couldn't seem to stop his meaningless chatter. "I was talking to him only a couple of hours ago," he said to no one in particular. "I can't believe it! He was standing in the hallway just outside the lab, smoking a cigar. 'How's the diet going?' he asked me. I told him at the seminar last week that I couldn't eat the cookies because my wife has put me on a high-protein diet."

David Shiloh was even more businesslike than usual. "There was a shattered bottle of mercaptoethanol," he informed them, referring to a reagent common in biochemistry labs. "If he had opened it, the stink would have covered the smell of the gas."

Alex was ten years younger than Yekeziel, and a good fifteen years younger than David Shiloh. He was slim and slightly above medium height, with straight dark brown hair and the kind of fair skin that tans quickly. Dark-lashed blue-gray eyes and high cheekbones were the distinctive features of a strikingly handsome face.

He went to stand in the doorway facing away from the room, trying to make sense of the fact that while Ilan had been blown to bits, his watch was still running. It had struck him for the first time when his father died: It was heaping insult on injury that a human being, even the best, was outlasted by things that no one gave a damn about after their owner was gone.

David and Yekeziel were still in the lab, by the telephone. "As for being harebrained, did you ever hear the Josephina story?" David asked. Yekeziel looked at him blankly.

"She was a master's student of mine," David went on, "and Ilan was a co-supervisor of her project. One day he took her to check her DNA gel, and they had it on the u.v. light box for a long time while he explained to her what all the fluorescent bands were."

"But he neglected to warn her not to stare at an ultraviolet light without protective glasses. Later her eyes began to hurt terribly, and in the evening her husband took her to the emergency room. When the doctor realized what had happened, he said, 'This is amazing! It's very rare to get a case of ultraviolet-burned retina, but we've had two this afternoon. A Professor Falk from the university was here two hours ago with a worse burn than yours!' "

At the funeral the following afternoon, the members of the department of molecular biology were still stunned by the sudden violent death. Although Professor Falk hadn't been especially well liked, he had been a familiar presence for quite a few years. Alex Kertész was one of those who had not particularly liked Ilan Falk; it wasn't for nothing that he had consigned him to hell just before he actually went there. The reason for this was that, prior to leaving the department to take up his postdoctoral fellowship in the U.S., Alex had asked Ilan's advice regarding a technique that he knew was used routinely in Ilan's lab.

Ilan quizzed Alex and had decided that the research problem was interesting and the approach Alex proposed very promising. "But why should you do that part of the experiment?" he had said. "My students do those assays all the time. We can easily run them for you. Why don't we make a joint project of it?"

Alex had accepted the offer of cooperation gladly. It would certainly be more efficient, and he could use the time saved to run additional experiments.

His predictions had turned out to be almost uncannily accurate, and the assays performed by Ilan's students, principally by Rafi Baum, became an important part of a good piece of work. Only it wasn't until just before Alex had to leave that Ilan found the time to sit down with him and write up the paper.

While Alex was in America they received a response from a prestigious British journal saying that the results were interesting and exciting, and that they would be pleased to publish it after some rewriting. That was when the trouble started. Ilan didn't like Alex's rewritten draft, and he couldn't find the time either to work on it with Alex or to produce his own version. By the time Alex returned as a lecturer, the equivalent of an assistant professor in America, nothing further had been done. Six months later Ilan was still stubbornly refusing to cooperate.

Alex was angry and frustrated, but there seemed to be nothing he could do about it. Sitting at his desk just before the explosion, he had come to the conclusion that the time had come to cut his losses. He would write up a shortened version of the paper, leaving out the data from Ilan's lab. A decent paper in a journal was better than a really good paper in Ilan Falk's desk drawer.

The service was held in the austere premises of the municipal funeral hall in Sanhedria. Now a residential neighborhood on the northeast side of Jerusalem, Sanhedria was once supposedly the seat of the Sanhedrin, the council of seventy-one wise men who formed the supreme court of ancient Israel. There were many ancient burial caves in the area, some of them in people's backyards. Interestingly, although it was a religious neighborhood, no one seemed to care that there were probably additional graves under the buildings. Let anything remotely resembling a grave be found at an archaeological site, however, even one from the Stone Age, and religious fanatics, no doubt also from the Stone Age, would set up a hue and cry about the desecration of Jewish bones that caused archaeologists to be stoned and the government to tremble.

After the service a large number of people accompanied the body to the cemetery at Givat Shaul, the hill named for Saul, the biblical king. Because of the contours of the hilly terrain, the view from Ilan's gravesite was limited to a seemingly endless array of vertical or horizontal tombstones. There were wilting bouquets of flowers on some of the horizontal slabs, and fresh carnations, left no more than a day ago, on one grave near where Alex stood. The small stones scattered on many of the graves meant that some mourners had wanted to leave this simple token of their visit to the deceased. Naturally, there were no statues or pictures anywhere: The Second Commandment expressly forbade both. The day was gray and chilly, and Alex was wondering why he had felt obliged to come.

When the body, wrapped in dark blue cloth, had been lowered into the grave, there was a pause while family members took a last look. Then the gravediggers began throwing in shovelfuls of earth, and Alex turned to leave.

He was stopped by Professor Nahum Bron. Nahum means "comforted," but the habitual sardonic grin on the sallow, weatherbeaten face never meant anything of the kind for those he picked as his verbal sparring partners.

"Well, Alex, I see you've come after all," he began, with an anticipatory glint in his eye. "I would have thought you would be more likely to murder him than to mourn at his funeral."

"The same thought occurs to me about you," Alex responded.

Nahum laughed appreciatively. He enjoyed having a reputation for wickedness. "But in your case I have something specific in mind," he said. "You were standing in the doorway of Ilan's office one day last week, and I heard you say to him, 'You won't accept anything I might write, you don't want to work on it together, and you don't have time to write it yourself. In other words, there's no way to publish this paper.' And Ilan said, 'It looks that way.' I was surprised you didn't clobber him on the spot, instead of walking away without saying a word. That's our Alex, I thought, always controlled, always courteous. It's no wonder that he's liked and respected by man, woman and child—though being young and handsome probably has something to do with it in the case of woman."

Surprisingly, these remarks were made with a warm smile that suggested that they weren't in the least ironic. Alex was more disconcerted by compliments from this unlikely source than he had been by the implied accusation of murder. It took him a moment to realize that he wasn't being praised ridiculously for the color of his eyes, or for having refrained from beating Ilan to death with a blunt instrument in the middle of the molecular biology department. Rather he had been honored with an offer of fatherly affection from a man he respected, a man who obviously didn't make such offers easily.

David Shiloh, slowly making his way back to the entrance of the cemetery, paused when he reached Nahum and Alex. Elisha Tal's bulk immediately filled the space beside David.

"What lies are you three telling about the departed?" Elisha demanded. "Anything that concerns me?"

Nahum gave him a sharp look, but David answered mildly for them all, "I still can't believe it. Such a tragedy for his family. And what an evening for us, eh, Alex? How about you, Elisha? Didn't you hear the explosion on our floor, or weren't you in the building at the time?"

"Are you kidding?" Elisha boomed. Several of the mourners turned to see what the commotion was about. "I was long gone by then! I've got much better things to do with my evenings than hang around the lab!" The last was said with a leer that made it clear that Elisha's every non-working minute was devoted to orgies that should cause lesser men like Nahum, David, and Alex to eat their hearts out with envy.

Nahum turned on his heel with a snort of disgust and walked away. David looked at his shoes in discomfort. Alex stared blankly at Elisha's back as he walked away. He had found Elisha's remarks odd in both content and context.

CHAPTER 2

Micky Warshavsky had the lab adjoining Alex's. He was a few years older and a little shorter, with a broad, powerful build, an open face, and mild brown eyes. As a student, he had made a good showing for Israel in international judo competitions. Although he had only joined the department during Alex's three-year stay in the United States, he had already been promoted to the position of senior lecturer and would no doubt be made a full professor in short order. To his credit, he was modest and unassuming in spite of his professional and athletic success.

He and his family often went hiking on Saturdays, and Alex had a standing invitation to join them, so he and Daniel, his eight-year-old son, spent many pleasant days with them exploring the countryside.

On the afternoon of the third day after Ilan Falk's funeral, Micky came into the lab where Alex and Arik, one of his students, were setting up an experiment.

"I'm on my way to pay a condolence visit to Geulah Falk," he said to Alex. "But it just occurred to me, suppose there's no one else there. I don't want to face her by myself! How about doing a good deed and coming with me?"

"I don't want to face her at all," Alex replied. "I hardly

know her. What about Adi?" he added, proposing that Micky's wife accompany him.

"We were planning to go together," Micky explained, "but she came down with the flu yesterday. She obviously isn't going to be well enough to go before the week of mourning is over. I have to pay my respects. We were friendly with Ilan and Geulah."

"Can you carry on here for an hour or so without Alex?" he asked Arik, hoping to get Alex out of the lab before he could think of an excuse.

Arik gave him a withering look. "I'll manage," he said.

Alex soon found himself in Micky's old blue Peugeot on the road out of Jerusalem, with the light-colored stone houses of Ramot, the city's northwestern neighborhood, spread over the hillside on the other side of the valley on their right. In a few minutes they were descending through the pine-studded hills of the Jerusalem Forest. When they reached the road's lowest point they immediately began the steep climb that would bring them to their destination. This section of the highway was known for the periodic fatal accidents that occurred when heavy trucks or buses traveling in the opposite direction lost their brakes on the way down.

Within twenty minutes they arrived at the semidetached house in Mevasseret Zion, the hilltop suburb about ten kilometers west of Jerusalem where Ilan had lived. The name could be translated as "bearing glad tidings of Zion." It was generally shortened to "Mevasseret," and at rush hours bore very sad tidings of traffic jams up to an hour long at the entrance to Jerusalem. The compensating advantages of living in Mevasseret were that it was quiet, with pleasant, tree-lined streets, and houses were less expensive than in the city.

Micky was glad that he had had the foresight to coopt Alex, since there was no one at the house except Geulah Falk and her married daughter, who had left her family at home in Haifa to spend the week with her mother. After they were introduced, the daughter thanked them for coming and barely said another word during their visit.

The Falks also had a son who had recently finished his compulsory military service. He had been at the funeral. Micky assumed that he must be somewhere around the house, since custom dictated that the immediate family stay at home during this week, but he was nowhere to be seen.

Geulah was still a pretty woman, but she looked older than her years. The sudden loss of her husband had left her stunned, and in spite of Micky's genuine friendly concern and Alex's sympathy it wasn't easy to carry on a conversation.

"We wanted to tell you how sorry we are," Micky began as they came in.

Geulah led them into the sunny living room and stopped in front of the modern white couch, too tired, or apathetic, to decide where they should all sit. She gave Micky a wan smile, then roused herself and turned toward Alex. "You were one of the ones who found him, weren't you?" she asked. "I kept meaning to talk to you at the funeral, but there were so many people. . . . And now I don't think I want to talk about it, after all." She grasped his hand briefly between two damp palms, then gestured toward a pair of armchairs. She seated herself on the couch, facing them across a narrow coffee table.

Alex was wildly uncomfortable. He had never exchanged more than a few words with the older woman, and he had never met the young one before. What could he find to say to them when they were suffering from such a fresh and terrible loss? Especially, how could he think of comforting words with the picture of Ilan's body still so vivid in his mind?

Micky was wonderful. "The last time I was here was in December," he reminisced, "when you invited the visiting Americans. It was a very nice evening, I remember, and Adi and I both thought that Ilan seemed to really be enjoying himself. He had a good year, didn't he?"

"Yes. Yes, I think that's true," Geulah agreed, giving the idea serious consideration. "His work was going well, and I'm sure he was happy."

"He spent a month in Copenhagen," the daughter put in, coming to life for the first and only time. "He always enjoyed that. He brought me some perfume from the airport."

"How is Adi?" Geulah asked after a short silence.

"She's got the flu," Micky told her. "Otherwise she certainly would have come." Geulah nodded and lapsed into silence.

It was while Micky and Alex were each waiting for the other to make the first move to leave that the doorbell rang, and Ilan's daughter admitted two uniformed policemen in visored caps and dark blue winter windbreakers. Geulah seemed to be unduly upset by their arrival, even before one of them enquired politely whether Oded Falk was at home. The young woman answered that her brother wasn't there, and in reply to further questioning, that she and her mother had no idea where he might be.

"You may not be aware that Professor Falk died just five days ago, and his wife and daughter are in mourning," Micky told the policemen severely.

The policemen exchanged glances. "No, we didn't know," one of them said. "That might change the situation, since I believe he was the one who made the accusation of auto theft. If there's no one to press charges, we may have to close the file."

"Yes!" Geulah exclaimed. "I mean, no, I certainly don't want to press charges. Please do close the file," she continued with quiet dignity. "My son hasn't committed any crime, and I would like the file to be closed as soon as possible."

After the policemen had left, Geulah seemed relieved to be able to tell them the story. The previous week Oded and his father had argued about something, and subsequently Ilan had refused to let Oded take the family car. There was no reason for his refusal other than pique. No one else needed the car. The young man, no less stubborn than his father, had driven off anyway, and Ilan had called the police and accused his son of stealing his car. Oded had been picked up driving a "stolen" vehicle, and now, if charges were pressed as his father had insisted on doing, he would be in serious trouble.

"In one respect at least, it was lucky for Oded that his dad died," Micky commented during the drive back to the university. "Maybe this business explains why I haven't seen him working in his father's lab lately. I assumed that he must have found a real job.

"Why the thoughtful silence, Alex?" Micky continued. "In the light of your own experience, I'm sure you're not surprised to hear that Ilan Falk could be a pig-headed bastard?"

"I didn't have the impression that he was a bastard," Alex said, "although I definitely subscribe to the pig-headed part. I didn't take what he did to me personally, I just thought he was making a mess of things. He took on too many projects at once, and he wanted complete control of all of them.

"Maybe he was trying to compete with younger people who were accomplishing more than he was. Like you. The maddening thing was that instead of organizing his time, he would wander up and down the hall, obviously doing absolutely nothing, complaining to anyone who would listen about how busy he was. I admit that I thought of a few choice names for him."

"What, for instance?" Micky asked, interested.

"They were all in Hungarian," Alex answered apologetically.

"No, really," Micky insisted. "He could be a bastard. Your trouble is that you're such a nice guy you can't imagine how nasty some people really are.

"Last Monday, two days before he died, he asked me to come into his office for a minute. Then he shut the door and told me he was considering writing a letter to the administrators of the Landon Prize, telling them that Elisha had faked the results that won him the prize. On what basis? Information he got from Elisha's wife! I told him that in my opinion, it would be unforgivable to make an accusation like that without being absolutely sure that it was true—after all, it would ruin the man's career! But he was too stubborn to admit that I was right."

Elisha had left his wife five months earlier to move in with one of his students. It wouldn't be surprising if she were willing to go to great lengths to get back at him.

"Even assuming that she wouldn't lie," Alex asked, "how would she know whether his experimental results were real or faked?"

"I suppose Elisha must have told her about the forgery when he did it. The paper that clinched the prize was published nearly two years ago, so he would have written it well before that, long before he left her. She doesn't have access to his notebooks anymore, of course, but she said that she knows exactly where the proof can be found. Ilan said she told him that a friend had advised her to tell him about it, because he would know what to do and would be sure to act."

CHAPTER 3

The following morning Rafi found Alex in his small office opposite the lab. There was enough room for the wooden desk in front of the window and also for two wooden chairs for visitors. One wall was taken up by books and the rapidly accumulating journals. Alex had subscriptions to *Science*, *The Journal of Bacteriology*, and *Microbiological Reviews*. *Science* let him glean whatever he could understand of the news from fields as far removed from his own as geology and astrophysics without leaving his chair, but it wasn't essential, and when his discount subscription expired he would do without it. He subscribed to the specialist journals because the small library in the biology building didn't get them.

Rafi had been Ilan Falk's best student. He had done most of the experiments Ilan had undertaken in connection with the ill-fated joint research project. Now, having finished his thesis work, Rafi was preparing to leave for a postdoctoral fellowship at Harvard. Or at least, he had been preparing to do that. He was already talking as he threw himself down on the chair facing the desk, oblivious of the fact that he was interrupting.

"I need your help," he announced. "Would you write a letter of recommendation for me to Tobias at Oxford?

Could you do it right away? Time is getting short, and I don't want to miss out there, too."

"Of course," Alex replied. "But what happened to Harvard?"

"Don't you know?" Rafi said bitterly. "My thesis adviser, who thought so highly of me, was supposed to send a letter of recommendation for me three months ago. But it seems he never did. Last week I got a letter from Kaplan saying that he couldn't keep the position for me any longer. He had to give a final reply to the other applicants. So now I have to move fast to make sure of the post with Tobias. I got through to him on the phone yesterday and he said the place is still available, but he won't wait long either. It's too bad. That project was exactly what I wanted to work on."

Rafi stared out the window over Alex's shoulder for a moment, then shook his head. "I couldn't believe it, when I got that letter. How could Ilan do that to me? What I couldn't forgive was the hypocrisy. When I first told him that Kaplan had accepted me, he made such a fuss about it. He told me what an honor it was for both me and the lab, and that it would make a big difference for my career. I guess he just couldn't stand to see someone else succeed.

"Well, that's that. Now I need some recommendations for Tobias, and you can say more about my work than most of the other faculty members because of the research we did together.

"Come to think of it," he added, brightening a little, "now that Ilan's gone, is there any reason why you can't revise the paper and send it off? Needless to say, I would be happy to cooperate in any way I can. Having my name on it would help make up for losing Kaplan. I know how anxious you were to get it out."

"I don't think there's any reason not to do that, now," Alex replied slowly. It had already occurred to him that he needn't mutilate the paper now that Ilan was out of the picture, but it bothered him that the idea gave him a completely uncalled-for pang of guilt. As Rafi left, he wondered whether there was anyone in the country who had not benefited by Ilan's death.

In the afternoon, Alex reached a stage in the DNA extraction he was performing when the samples had to be left on ice. He took advantage of it to spend an hour at the weekly departmental seminar, held in one of the classrooms at the end of the corridor. After helping themselves to the instant coffee and cookies the department provided, the audience filed into the lecture room and seated themselves in the one-armed schoolroom chairs.

The lecturer this week was Professor Elisha Tal, who was to present the results of his recent research on the biochemistry of leukemic blood cells. All the members of his research group had come, including Nina, the tall, dark-haired woman who was his technician. Naturally, Orli was there. She was the attractive young woman student who everyone knew was Elisha's mistress. She had done some of the experimental work that was to be reported.

Although everyone in the department knew of the relationship that the pair made no attempt to disguise, no one could understand it, since Elisha was paunchy and middle-aged and had the face of a bad-tempered pig. It was accepted that a sensitive person might be attracted by inner beauty, but Elisha showed no detectable sign of such a quality either. In fact, he was vulgar, boastful, aggressive, and rude.

The research he described was quite interesting. It involved a protein thought to be specific to leukemic blood cells and being considered as the basis for a new diagnostic test. He claimed to have found an identical protein in cells of a completely different type. For one thing, an extract of the second type of cell could mimic the effect of his leukemic cell protein. Also, the antibody to the protein from leukemic cells seemed to absorb one of the minor proteins from the crude extract of the second cell type. This was shown by the apparent disappearance of one of the protein bands of the extract, made visible by a technique known as PAGE (polyacrylamide gel electrophoresis).

He concluded by saying that although his evidence was still highly circumstantial, he believed that he had discovered the purported leukemia protein in a previously unsuspected type of cell. If he was right, the presence of this protein in blood wasn't necessarily associated with leukemia. The information would be very important to researchers looking for better ways to diagnose blood cancer.

"After you've absorbed the protein out of the nonleukemic cell extract with your antibody," Alex asked, "does the extract still mimic the effect of the leukemia protein?"

Elisha's momentary stunned silence made it obvious that he hadn't thought of this simple experiment that could immediately prove his case. "He's right, Elisha," David Shiloh exclaimed. "That would settle the question right away."

"Of course. It's neat and simple. I would do that first thing," Micky Warshavsky said. Several other members of the audience chimed in with similar remarks. By this time Elisha had recovered himself and responded with what everyone realized was a bold-faced lie.

"Naturally, that experiment is already being done in my lab," he said. "I don't need you to tell me what to do, Alex." His booming voice rose. "Who the hell do you think you are? You conceited young ass! You—" He was working himself up into a towering rage. Then he noticed his colleagues' shocked faces, and he restrained himself with obvious effort.

Catching up with Alex in the hallway after the seminar, he said, "You insulted me in front of the whole department, Alex, suggesting that I'm too stupid to know how to run my own research. That was a big mistake. I want you to know that I'm not as stupid as a junior lecturer who makes an enemy of me. I won't forget this." This time it was Alex who was left in stunned silence as Elisha barreled past him.

Would this sort of intimidation prevent him from commenting on Elisha's work in the future, he wondered? No, of course not. Human nature being what it was, it was more likely to make him find fault where there was none on the next occasion.

A response such as Elisha's stripped the departmental seminar of its value as a forum for discussion. In this case he had also injected a jarring personal note to spoil a purely cerebral pleasure. Alex was about to mentally consign Elisha to an appropriate place when he caught himself up short. After his recent experience, when Ilan Falk had gone directly to hell as soon as he had wished him there, perhaps he should be more careful with wishes of this sort. Alternatively he might consider giving them free rein and performing a useful service for the department by expeditiously removing its most insufferable members.

He gave no more thought to Elisha as he continued with the DNA isolation. He needed to obtain a particular plasmid, an independent unit of circular DNA. This plasmid contained the genes for some proteins that were toxic to specific insect species. It was his second attempt to prepare enough of this DNA for cloning, and he hoped it would be more successful than his first. As on many previous occasions, he thought wistfully of those lucky people who worked with E. coli. Plasmid preps from that bacterium never failed, while extracting a giant plasmid from a bacillus seemed to depend more on serendipity than on any factor under the control of the experimenter.

After a few hours of work, Alex took a mug with instant coffee powder and sugar in it to the "coffee room" at the end of the hall to get hot water from the big electric kettle. This was the only room in the department where eating and drinking was officially sanctioned. It was thought that eating and drinking in the laboratories could lead to sandwiches spiced with radioactive or other exotic material. An absentminded scientist might even pick up the wrong cup and take a swig of cyanide before he realized his mistake. But keeping food out of the labs would have been a major inconvenience, because lots of sandwiches were eaten during work in that building. There was a cafeteria with edible food, but it was at the other end of the campus. There was also a more expensive restaurant closer by. It was supposedly a faculty club, but actually it was democratically open to anyone whose stomach could take it.

There was probably no one who didn't at least drink in the laboratory, in spite of the proliferation of posted warnings. The little signs that kept popping up must have served the purpose of relieving the administration of responsibility for any accident. They certainly couldn't have seriously expected compliance with warnings not to enter the lab without a lab coat, not to leave the room in a lab coat, not to keep chemicals in the room and not to spill any in the sink, and—there were several signs on each door for this most irrelevant admonition—to wear safety goggles at all times.

Keeping food out of the labs was one of the more reasonable demands, but it wasn't really necessary in most cases. As a practical matter, no harm had ever come from ignoring it. Alex himself had accidentally tasted various disgusting, corrosive, or radioactive liquids in the course of his work, but it had generally been because he was working under the pressure of time, without the proper equipment. It had certainly never been because he mistook them for his coffee.

The coffee room was furnished with a few low, imitation wood tables and armless upholstered chairs of the kind found in dentists' waiting rooms. The walls were decorated with a collection of old drawings of birds that someone had donated to the university. The once bright colors had faded and the paper had turned yellow. They were always askew. People did tend to gather there, but Alex usually just took advantage of the constant supply of boiling water and drank his coffee in his office or the lab.

When he entered the coffee room he startled the only person there so much that she dropped her full cup. It shattered on the vinyl floor, splashing coffee in all directions. Alex apologized, although he hadn't done anything except open the door. The clumsy coffee-drinker was a slender young woman with hazel eyes and long, shining honey-colored hair tied in a casual ponytail. She was a research assistant in Ilan Falk's lab. Alex didn't know much about her except that she had a dark, glowering husband who would sometimes pick her up from work. He also knew that he enjoyed looking at her. Although Alex didn't know this, her given name was Lilliana, which was why everyone called her Shosh. Shoshana is sometimes translated as lily, and Shosh is short for Shoshana, so it was perfectly logical.

"It wasn't your fault," Shosh told him, with a sad little smile that was not at all like the usual quiet cheerfulness that was one of the attractive things about her. "How stupid not to be able to hold on to a cup. My nerves are in a worse state than I thought."

His inquiring look seemed to bring her to a decision. "Do you have a few minutes?" she asked finally. "I want to tell this to someone."

"Yes, of course," he replied, wondering why she didn't tell her husband whatever it was. He immediately chided himself for the thought, reminding himself how unlikely it was that he would confide in his wife.

They had wiped up the worst of the mess, and Alex sat down facing her across the low table over his still unfilled mug. He noticed that the olive-green sweater that she wore with her faded blue jeans reflected the color of her eyes.

"I'm afraid that I killed Ilan," she said abruptly, looking steadily into the clear light eyes that were focused on hers because he was listening intently.

"You mean it was you who left the gas jet open on the day he died?" Alex asked.

"No," she replied. "That's not what I mean. I wasn't even in Jerusalem on the day he died—I had some vacation coming, and we spent four days with friends who have an apartment in Eilat."

Alex waited silently for her explanation.

"I think I killed him by wishing it," she said hesitantly. "Do you believe that's possible? The thing is, I hated Ilan. He used to exploit me, browbeat me, and humiliate me. It was awful working for him, but Avi has been out of work for a long time, and I needed the job. They're not so easy to find.

"Then he decided that I wasn't staying late enough—he himself wasn't here at all half the time, but he wanted to be able to pop in at ten o'clock at night and find everyone at work. So he was going to fire me! And when I said it wasn't fair, that I had been working very hard, and that he was going to present a paper based entirely on my work in Greece next month, he got mad and told me he would prevent me from getting any other job, too. He would tell anyone who asked for a reference that I was stupid and lazy."

Alex relaxed and leaned back. "Then I can understand why you wished him dead," he told her. "But that doesn't make you responsible for it. Or at least, we share the responsibility," he suggested, wanting to lighten her mood, "because I was wishing him to hell only a moment before the explosion."

She shook her head impatiently. "That's not all. I wished him to die exactly as he did! I thought, He's so careless. He could easily leave the gas on some day and light one of those smelly cigars. Wouldn't that be great!

"And there's something else," she rushed on, as if to tell the whole crazy story before she lost her nerve. "In Eilat, the night he died, I had a very strange dream. I dreamed that I had killed someone, only the body hadn't been found yet. It was in a locked room. But I knew it was going to be discovered the next day. In the dream, I was answering the question, would I be sorry for killing this man when the body was discovered? The answer was no! I would be glad I had done it! The next day I came back to the lab and heard about Ilan," she concluded.

"Jézus, Mária!" Alex said softly. He had acquired the expression from his father, a volatile man who had used it often.

"You see!" Shosh said.

An hour later Alex finally left the precipitated samples that might or might not contain DNA, threw on his jacket, and ran down the stairs.

He was walking rather slowly through the parking lot toward his car, thinking about Shosh's remarkable dream, when he heard the roar of an engine behind him. Without taking the time to turn around he hurled himself at the side of the building, crashing painfully into the stone wall.

The car passed within inches, then screeched to a stop, and Elisha's head appeared at the open window as he leaned over from the driver's side. "Ha Ha! You looked just like a scared rabbit! You had nothing to worry about, sonny, I was only going to tickle you a bit. I'm a very good driver, you know—I used to be a fighter pilot!" He gunned the engine and sped off.

Varda looked up from the sketch she was studying when Alex opened the door of their apartment. She was wearing a bright pink sweater, and with her hair, the color of ripe strawberries, cascading over her shoulders, she reminded him of the sunrise on a beautiful morning. She was also as far away. All his love had not been sufficient to keep hers, if he had ever had it, and finally her stony indifference had worn his own feeling down to nothing. But if he had stopped caring years ago, why did the sight of her still bring these thoughts to mind, and why were they always so painful?

"Good god!" Varda said as she raised her head. "What have you done to your face?"

"I ran into a wall," he told her. She was looking at him uncertainly, so he explained. "Elisha Tal was trying to run me over."

With a brief skeptical glance she went back to her sketches, and he said no more about it.

Alex was standing with his back to the door, weighing out agarose for a minigel to check his plasmid preparation, when Nina, Elisha Tal's technician, came in and stood at his elbow. "Good morning, Alex," she said, with a toss of her head. The toss was presumably to throw the heavy waves of black hair out of her eyes, but it had become an annoying mannerism, since she repeated it every few minutes whether or not there was need for it.

"Good morning, Nina," he replied, turning to face her. "Can I help you?"

"I wanted to tell you how awful I think Elisha was at the seminar yesterday," she said earnestly. "The way he spoke to you was really inexcusable! I wouldn't want you to think that I condone his behavior, just because I'm part of his group."

"Of course not," Alex replied.

She stepped closer and lowered her voice conspiratorially. "I also wanted to warn you to be careful," she said. "He won't forgive you for a long time. I have a feeling that he may try to do something to get back at you."

He resisted the impulse to retreat to a comfortable speaking distance, and waited for her to explain herself. During the pause she stared at his face. "He hit you, didn't he!"

she said with a new light in her eyes and a strange little smile.

"No," he replied shortly. Strictly, it was true. He could have sworn that the expression that came over her face was disappointment.

"Oh. Well, why don't we have coffee together sometime?" she said. With a final toss of her head, she was gone.

As he finished weighing out the chemical, Alex recalled two figures from his childhood. There had been a miserable creature named András in the class ahead of his, a puny boy too small to achieve the power he craved on his own. So he had become the slavish follower of the school bully. The bully's name was Sándor, the Hungarian version of Alexander, the same as Alex's. But everyone called him by the nickname Sani, which they pronounced Shawnee. Alex had an irrational but strong dislike for the nickname, and had managed to avoid it by refusing to answer to it. He hadn't thought much of a bully who would let himself be called Sani, but this opinion was held from a distance, since he hadn't had much contact with the bigger boy.

He had been walking home from school, kicking a pebble along in front of him, when the sudden movement of a shadow above and to his right made him twist away. In the next instant a powerful glancing blow on his right shoulder ripped his shirt and nearly sent him flying. He had concentrated all his efforts on regaining his balance, and after stumbling a few steps had managed to right himself and turned to face his attacker.

Sani was standing in front of him with the weapon again held above his head, and Alex had been shocked to see that it was a heavy, weatherbeaten plank with a rusty nail protruding from the end. If that nail had been brought down on his head it would have killed him.

Behind Sani cowered the despicable András. That was where Alex had previously seen the expression of guilty excitement that had crossed Nina's face.

"Hit him, Sani! Hit him again!" András had yelled, with the same excitement in his eyes, the same avid smile.

It wasn't surprising that now, so many years later, he couldn't remember why Sani had been in such a murderous rage. Neither could he remember what it was about the incident that had continued to trouble him for a long while afterward.

By evening Alex knew that his second plasmid preparation was no more successful than the first. He was slouched in the wooden chair at the desk in the alcove off the lab with his legs stretched out in front of him, tired and if not depressed, not cheerful either.

"What's this? Why aren't you working?" Micky asked jovially as he wandered in. "No one ever won a Nobel Prize by lying around!"

"No one ever won a Nobel Prize by working, either, if he couldn't get even a few nanograms of plasmid out of a bug," Alex replied without moving. "I was thinking of drinking a cup of Elite instant coffee and putting myself out of my misery," he added, mentioning the prevalent brand. "Are you tempted to join me?"

"No," Micky said decisively. "I've had better offers than that even within the last five minutes. Wait a minute," he called on his way out the door. "I've got something that will put you out of your misery much less painfully." He returned with a bottle of cherry liqueur and his coffee mug, picked up Alex's empty mug from the desk where it stood amid a litter of books and papers, and poured out a swig for each of them. "Tami brought this for the lab when she came back from Germany," he said.

Alex took a small sip and made a face. "It's as awful as I remember," he said. "Why do people buy this stuff? It tastes just like cough medicine!"

"The authentic Israeli considers this 'stuff' to be the epitome of drinking sophistication," Micky said in a superior tone. "I suppose as a Hungarian you would prefer something that makes smoke come out of your ears, and as a Frenchman something with no sugar, that makes your tongue cleave to the roof of your mouth. But you're in Israel now, so drink up!"

Alex was the son of a Hungarian doctor who had been the head surgeon at a large hospital in Budapest, and a Jewish Frenchwoman who had gone to Hungary to teach in the early fifties.

Because of the gratitude of a powerful patient, Alex's father had once been allowed to attend a medical conference abroad, taking his wife and children along. That was how it happened that they were with him in Paris at the time of his fatal heart attack, when Alex was sixteen. His mother had wanted them to stay there, where she had relatives, rather than go back to communist Hungary now that their father would no longer be there. His sister, who was a ballet dancer, could continue her training and would perhaps be able to join a ballet troupe in Paris, and he could finish high school and study at the Sorbonne.

They had agreed to leave behind friends, relatives, and possessions and to escape the Dictatorship of the People. In the end, though, he'd gone to Israel after only one year of university and continued his studies at the University of Jerusalem after completing his army service.

Alex laughed and took a few more sips of the syrupy liquid. "Now it's a challenge," he said. "But if I learned to drink 'mud' and Elite instant coffee I can learn to drink this too." "Mud" was a horrible concoction made by pouring boiling water over fine coffee grounds and drinking the result without further treatment. Drinking it is the first skill a recruit of the Israeli army must acquire, if he doesn't already have it.

"Actually," he commented, "it doesn't seem so bad, after you've drunk some. But I don't think I'm ever going to develop a taste for it."

Now that they were seated facing each other, Micky asked, "What happened to your face? It looks like you ran into a wall!"

"I did," Alex replied. "I was dodging Elisha. He tried to run me over in the parking lot last night."

"To run you over!" Micky repeated idiotically. "He must have been planning it all afternoon, then, because he's always gone by four at the latest. He must have waited for you to leave. The man's not normal!"

"He said he was only planning to graze me. He used to be a fighter pilot, and is therefore a very good driver."

"Fighter pilot, my foot! He used to be an officer in the

tank corps, but he was demoted for beating a recruit nearly to death. Nahum told me about it quite a while ago, and someone else I know confirmed it." After a moment's thought he added, "He seems to take things personally."

They looked at each other in silence, the same thought having occurred to each of them: If Elisha had reacted with such violence to an imaginary insult from Alex, what would he have done if he had known about a real threat to his career from Ilan Falk? Alex was the one to voice it. "I wonder if he knew about that letter Ilan was going to send?"

"Good question," Micky replied. "Do you think there's any way we could ask him that?"

"Maybe there's some way you could ask him," Alex said morosely. "As for me—if he sees me first, I probably won't have much time for asking questions."

CHAPTER 5

That March was a wet month, and since Saturday was another cold, rainy day, Alex took advantage of the opportunity to visit Yehudit and Akiva. The couple were the parents of Uri, the first friend he had made in Israel when he had arrived at the age of nineteen and joined the army. He and Uri had gone through basic training together, and afterward had served in the same unit.

It had been a lonely year. When he had come to Israel and volunteered for the paratroops he hadn't realized what it would mean to come to a country where he knew no one and didn't even speak the language. Not that he had regretted the impulse, a reaction to his encounter with the Sorbonne. He didn't know what he had expected of the French university, certainly not Plato's academy, but the reality had depressed and dismayed him.

It had been the students who disappointed him, with their simplistic world view and a facile Marxism that was impervious to reason. They would concede that socialism as practiced in the Communist Bloc wasn't perfect and that a few mistakes might have been made, but beyond that, they toed the Party line.

They refused to accept the evidence of his experience, because it conflicted with the judgment of the ivory-tower experts who sat in their offices in Paris and turned out articles for *Le Monde*. With those fantastic articles as their bible, the students would spend endless evenings ranting against the bourgeoisie and arguing the finer points of a system about which they didn't understand the most basic facts.

There were a few who had a different point of view. One evening, at a party, a girl said to him, "I think communism is stupid and perverse. I'm sure that you agree."

"No, I don't," he replied. "I try to be objective about the theory, even though I've seen how badly it can work out in practice."

"Oh, in practice, there's no difference between here and Eastern Europe," she had said. "After all, France is also a police state."

As he searched the pretty, blank face for some sign that she understood what she was saying, fragments of scenes from Budapest flashed through his mind. The dingy, decaying buildings that must once have been beautiful. The old woman, like a black widow spider, who was the concierge of the apartment building where his family lived. She was an informer for the AVH, the secret police, and had accused his mother of being a French spy. The idea was ridiculous, but when they picked him up as he left his high school, he didn't feel like laughing.

The small office to which they took him was perfectly ordinary and very frightening. The fear the AVH inspired was of a particular kind, characteristic of police states. It stemmed from the knowledge of their unchecked power. Life could be very hard for those unlucky enough to attract their attention. Even if there was never an official accusation of any sort, a career could be ruined. A home could be reassigned to some one else. Schools would have no openings, and travel documents would be unavailable. Useless to visit government offices; no one would know who was responsible, or why these things had happened. At least in this case he knew who had caused the trouble.

His repeated denials of any antistate activities by his mother only made them impatient. The two who "interviewed" him weren't interested in finding out whether or not his mother was guilty—they assumed that she was. They only wanted to hear him confirm it so the state could take its revenge.

They believed that his mother had dealings with an enemy agent. The "agent" was one of the few Western tourists, a Frenchwoman who had apparently wandered onto their street by mistake, and asked the concierge for directions. It was the concierge herself who had called his mother to speak to the woman in French. Unfortunately the woman returned the next day to look for his mother. Since she wasn't home, the woman left a French magazine for her with the concierge.

Of course they already knew about his mother's correspondence with the aunt in Paris who was her closest living relative. It went without saying that the letters from both sides were read by the AVH, so his mother was careful to say nothing that could be considered political. That didn't leave much, but it was important to his mother to stay in touch.

The letters were addressed to "Dear Aunt Yvette," and referred to nothing but husband and children. But how did the AVH know that "Aunt Yvette" was really an old lady in Paris? And "husband" and "children" could be code words for anything. The repeated references to "hospital" were especially suspicious. It was true that her husband worked in a hospital, but the AVH knew very well that "hospital" was often used by antistate criminals to refer to an army camp or prison.

And his father should realize that his antisocialist and undemocratic opinions hadn't gone unnoticed. He shouldn't count too heavily on the fact that certain so-called medical experts considered him irreplaceable.

Mrs. Nagy, the concierge, had often heard Alex speaking French with his mother in a secretive way. Probably they were all in it together. Who was "Aunt Yvette"? What information was his mother passing to her French contacts?

It was like being trapped in a nightmare. They asked the same questions over and over, trying to make him give answers that he didn't have. The bigger one, a mountain of a man, twisted Alex's arm behind his back so hard that another millimeter would have broken his elbow.

"I'm sorry that I have to do this," he said. "But it's for your own good; like being punished by the teacher when you tell lies in school. I can keep this up all day," he added, "so why don't you just tell us now what you're going to tell us anyway, sooner or later, and then you can go home?"

The slender one with the little mustache sat at his desk and watched intently. When he got up, it was to smooth the hair back from Alex's forehead and stroke his cheek with a clammy hand. Alex imagined that it left a track like a snail. He squeezed the shoulder of Alex's free arm.

"I like you," he said. "I don't want to hurt you. I'm sure you're not guilty of any serious crime. But your parents are a bad influence." He smiled ingratiatingly, his hand still resting on Alex's shoulder. "I can be your friend," he said, "if you'll let me."

"You may think your arm is broken," the big one explained, "but it isn't. When a bone snaps it makes a nice, cracking sound."

Alex stopped responding to their questions. He didn't know what else to say, and the combination of pain and caresses confused him.

They described what they could do to various parts of his anatomy if he refused to cooperate. He was supposed to be scared to death, and no doubt he would have been, except that the threats were so bizarre that he couldn't take them seriously. His fellow Hungarians had come a long way, after all, since the days of their revered ancestor Attila the Hun. And the unrelenting pressure on his arm made it hard to worry about relatively minor discomforts like having his ears ripped off or his genitals sliced away.

He wondered what would happen next. After they broke his arm, then what? Would they think that they might do better with his mother? Would the slight one fondle her with his sweaty hands? Would the big one slowly and painfully break her arm? He was suddenly filled with rage at the wicked old woman.

"You're going after the wrong person!" he said. "The spy you're looking for is Mrs. Nagy."

He pointed out that only Mrs. Nagy had spoken with the French "agent" in private. Twice, according to her own account. They had only Mrs. Nagy's word for it that the woman didn't speak Hungarian, and that she herself didn't understand a word of French. Actually, he told them, he had suspected for a long time that Mrs. Nagy understood French, because he had noticed her listening to his conversations with his mother.

If Mrs. Nagy hadn't called her, his mother would never have met the foreigner. Mrs. Nagy knew that because his mother was French, she could be used to divert suspicion.

It was a flimsy structure, but he delivered it with a cold fury that probably sounded like deep conviction. Mustache was impressed, at any rate. He smiled approvingly at Alex.

"That's a very interesting idea!" he said. "We'll have to look into it. You really are an intelligent boy. We could use your talents, if you would be willing to serve your country. You know, just meeting with us once in a while, and mentioning whatever you happened to notice among your classmates. Sad to say, several of them have parents who are Class Enemies, maybe even worse than your father. You would be doing a service for your family, too. Having a son who is a true patriot would make up for some of your parents' mistakes."

Alex felt the blood rushing from his face. His head seemed to spin, and nausea suddenly rose from the pit of his stomach. He was afraid that he was going to fall over.

"Let him go, you fool! Can't you see he's passing out?" Mustache said sharply.

The big one released his arm and caught him by the shoulders to keep him upright until he recovered his balance. Mustache managed to throw his arms around him also, although there was no need or room for both of them. He was literally locked in the embrace of the AVH. He thought that what nauseated him wasn't the pain in his arm but the realization that he had somehow become an AVH informer himself, little better than Mrs. Nagy.

He found himself on the street, at least temporarily still in possession of both his mother and his right arm. Maybe they hadn't believed the old woman in the first place. For all he knew, the experience that had turned him inside out had been a routine probe.

He flew home, hoping that there was time to warn the others. To his relief, his parents and his sister were there. His mother and father began hurried consultations. As they spoke his father was already putting on his overcoat, preparing to hunt down the most influential person he could think of.

It wasn't important that there was no evidence that his mother had ever done anything even remotely harmful to the Hungarian People's Republic. What mattered was whether his father knew someone who knew someone in the AVH who outranked the person the spiteful old woman reported to.

He tried to make himself inconspicuous, so they wouldn't waste time worrying about his arm. Later his father bandaged it. It was more than a week before he could stand to move it. He had trouble doing the simplest things during that time, and he got no sympathy from his cynical classmates. Instead they teased him unmercifully because he insisted that he had fallen down the stairs.

His family waited tensely during the next few weeks, but no one bothered them. Alex was afraid that he would see "them" waiting for him every time he left school, but they never came. Within the year his father was dead and they had left Hungary. They were able to forget about it. Almost. He knew that he didn't have the same reaction to the sight of a policeman as did his friends who had grown up in France.

He and this girl might have been from different planets. Although they both spoke French, there was no hope of communication. She was beginning to look uncomfortable, and he realized that he had been staring at her. "Excuse me," he had said abruptly, and walked away.

How was one to talk to these people, he had asked himself? Half the world was either enslaved or dying of starvation or both, and they chanted slogans against the "bosses" and saw themselves as a persecuted avant garde in a country where they were free to do whatever they liked. Those were the years when they could have been doing something useful, but instead they were wasting them arguing about the political equivalent of how many angels can dance on the head of a pin. By the end of the year he had decided to leave the Sorbonne and go to Israel to serve in the army.

* * *

The day he met Varda he had just arrived in Jerusalem on leave, intending to meet Uri at his parents' apartment in the evening. In the meantime, he went into a café and found a table where he could shove his kitbag out of the way and lean his rifle against the wall. The rifle was an awkward appurtenance, but each soldier was responsible for his weapon at all times so he had to keep it with him.

He was engrossed in a letter from home while he drank his coffee, and he didn't notice the girl who sat and sketched him on the other side of the room until she approached and held the drawing out for him to see.

"Jézus, Mária!" he had exclaimed. "I look like a boy who has just buried his dog!" The drawing, a perfect likeness, depicted a good-looking young man with light-colored eyes and neatly combed straight dark hair. He was in army uniform with his sleeves rolled up to his elbows and his beret tucked under his epaulet. He was holding a letter in his hand and looking up from it with an expression that clearly reflected the homesickness Alex had felt.

The artist, a striking red-haired girl with a proud stance and challenging green eyes, pulled up a chair and sat down across from him, leaning her white arms on the table. "You can have it if you like," she said.

"Oh, no, thank you," Alex answered. "I have nothing to do with it." Although the sketch was very well done, he certainly didn't want it himself, and with that expression on his face, he couldn't send it home either. Varda had introduced herself, explaining that she was studying art at the Bezalel Academy. When she had extracted the reason for his refusal to take the drawing, she offered to do another with any expression he chose.

"Come back with me to where I live," she suggested. "I have a compulsion to draw people lately, and you have a surprisingly expressive face. I'm sure your mother would like to have a good drawing of you."

Since he had no family in Israel, Uri's friendship and his parents' hospitality had been especially important. Alex had kept up the contact, and would drop in from time to time to see the parents in their Jerusalem apartment even after Uri moved to Netanya. Then Israel had gone to war in Lebanon and both he and Uri had been called up, though no longer serving in the same unit.

The war, unlike previous ones, was avoidable and un-necessary, in his opinion. It had none the less cost him six months lost from his doctoral research and much physical suffering. But Uri had lost his life, and his parents had lost their only child.

On his return from the postdoctoral fellowship in the United States Alex had renewed his habit of dropping in on Saturday afternoon with Daniel, his little boy. Some-times he would meet Uri's widow and child on a visit from Netanya, and occasionally various friends and neighbors. They all knew that Yehudit liked having guests and always baked a delicious cake on Friday for the benefit of those who would drop in the next day.

Yehudit and Akiva lived in Yemin Moshe, named for Sir Moses Montefiore, the British Jewish philanthropist.

Alex parked in the lot off King George Street at the highest point of the hillside neighborhood, near the old stone windmill. Akiva had told him that the windmill was used as an observation post by the Jewish fighters during the siege of Jerusalem in the War of Independence. The British authorities, trying to help the Arab side, blew the top off to make it useless. Akiva called that action "Operation Don Quixote."

Daniel ran down the stone steps that led to Yehudit and Akiva's street and along the narrow lane to their row house. Alex had to exert himself to keep up, even though his legs were much longer. Daniel would be very fast when he was grown. Alex wasted a moment hoping that he would live to see it.

When they reached Akiva's front porch they paused by mutual consent to look at the walls of the Old City, crowned by the conical green dome of the Dormition church, that rose atop the facing slope.

The Yemin Moshe neighborhood had fallen into decay during the years when its residents were a handy target for Jordanian snipers shooting down from the crenellated walls, but was rebuilt after 1967. The property suddenly became very valuable, so to prevent rampant speculation the right to buy was allocated by a lottery. It was lucky for Akiva that he was an engineer: When he won the option on a lot, he found the money to rebuild the old house by doing most of the work himself.

The living room, the same one Alex used to visit with Uri over ten years before, still held the same simple, well-worn furniture and faded imitation Persian carpet. Yehudit had filled every corner with potted plants and the walls were lined with many hundreds of Akiva's books, some old and hardbound with faded titles, others new paperbacks. They were in several languages and on a startling variety of subjects.

Akiva was as tall as Alex, lean and muscular, with a shock of gray hair. He prided himself on his strength, and to demonstrate it would shake hands with a bone-crushing grip that was painful if not anticipated. Long familiar with this pecadillo, Alex automatically braced himself for the encounter as soon as he had kissed Yehudit on the cheek in the doorway and entered the room. Daniel also knew what to expect—he was to be tossed in the air just as if he were a baby, and not a big boy of eight.

Yehudit had twinkling brown eyes in a broad Slavic face, and would have looked younger than her years if the thick hair pulled into a bun at the nape of her neck hadn't been completely white. She wore a light blue crocheted vest over a gray wool skirt and an immaculate starched white blouse.

"I must have known you were coming today," she told Daniel, "because I baked your favorite cake." She bustled off immediately to bring the chocolate cake with a chocolate glaze icing and nuts on top.

Daniel also had another piece of luck. Some neighbors, Mina and Elchanan, came in with their grandson, so he had someone to play with. Alex had met this couple a few times on previous visits, and he knew that they were both psychologists. They were unusually down to earth compared with other psychologists he had met, so even though their respective specialties were sexual counseling and educational testing, he dared to ask their opinions on a subject that had recently forced itself upon him.

"I've been wondering about the phenomenon of ill-wishing," he said when an opening presented itself, taking the plunge for lack of a better way to introduce the topic. "I know various primitive tribes believe in it, but have psychologists ever investigated it? Do you know whether anyone has tried to test whether it's possible to cause death or illness to someone by wishing it?"

"You can't be serious!" Mina exclaimed so sharply that her iron gray curls bounced. She was the specialist in educational testing, and apparently a little too down to earth for a question as strange as this. "I thought you were a scientist!"

Her husband, a plump, balding man with bright brown eyes behind gold-rimmed glasses, looked at Alex sharply. "I don't know of any psychological studies on the subject," he said. "Why do you ask?"

"Someone at work died recently," Alex told him, "and it seems that half of Jerusalem wished him dead. I wonder if all that concentrated thought could have had some effect."

Akiva cleared his throat, a sign that his mental encyclopedia contained some relevant entries. "The Australian aborigines believe very strongly in the efficacy of ill-wishing," he reported. "Also many African tribes. But they don't believe in the power of pure thought so much as in complicated rituals, such as finding some possession of the desired victim, or hair or fingernails from his body, or even his leftover food, and doing all sorts of nasty things to it.

"In one tribe in New Guinea, for instance, they take something from the victim and wrap it in a leaf that caterpillars eat, with the idea that in the same way the whole body will be eaten by worms. Then they put it in a piece of bamboo and wrap it with tree bark that's swollen, or smells bad. Then they wrap that with a creeper that withers very fast, and another one that's prickly. Then they wrap the whole thing in a withered leaf of the breadfruit tree, so the victim will wither and fall."

Yehudit lost patience with the outlandish habits of the aborigines and began to clear away the dishes. The others listened with rapt attention.

"They have to recite certain things," Akiva told them, "such as, 'May his limbs writhe in pain. May his whole body writhe in pain. May his entrails be contracted in pain. May his generative organs be distorted in pain. May he fall and rot like the gherkins!' "

"Gherkins?" Mina repeated.

"I looked it up. It's a kind of pickle."

Elchanan, the sex counselor, was nonplussed. "Where in the world did you get all that?" he asked.

"I read a very interesting book about it once," Akiva explained, "while I was a student at the university in Bratislava."

Alex didn't waste time being amazed at Akiva's vast store of knowledge, which didn't come as a surprise to him. He leaned forward in his chair, and the interest he took in the subject made his gray eyes glow as if a lamp had been lit behind them.

"I can picture a very serious anthropologist carefully noting all those details, but it's too much! I wonder if he didn't miss the forest for the trees."

"What is the forest, in your opinion?" Elchanan and Akiva asked more or less together.

"That it's the thought that's effective, and all those trappings only serve to help concentrate thought on the victim. In time they simply became traditional."

Elchanan and Akiva, and especially Mina, continued to look dubious, so he tried again. "Imagine a witchdoctor from New Guinea coming to observe how we cure the sick. If he accompanied Mina, let's say, to her local clinic, he would see that she first sits in a waiting room with a lot of other people. So he might decide that sick people in this country think it helps to gather together, the more the better.

"Then she goes in to see a doctor wearing a ceremonial costume—a white coat. After hearing her complaint, the doctor puts some tubes in his ears and taps her chest and back with a round silver object to which these tubes are connected—what a fascinating piece of ritual!

"He may wrap a bladder around her upper arm and pump it up with a little bulb, still with tubes in his ears. Maybe he'll peer into her mouth and ears with a little gadget that lights up, or stick a glass tube under her tongue and make her hold it for a minute.

"Finally, he scrawls some illegible marks on a slip of paper and says, 'I'm giving you penicillin,' or maybe 'erythromycin.' She takes the paper gratefully, and by the next day she feels much better. If the witchdoctor knew nothing about our medicine, how would he know what it was that actually cured her?"

"He wouldn't, of course," Elchanan agreed, taking off his glasses and wiping them absentmindedly. He turned his nearsighted gaze on Alex. "It's a thought-provoking analogy, but it's a long way from proving your case."

Yehudit had returned to her place on the couch beside Akiva in time to hear this recital. "It's true that our doctors aren't all that different from witchdoctors," she commented. "Especially when you go to them with something they don't know how to cure. Only then it isn't funny."

"If any such effects existed," Mina argued with Alex, "surely someone other than Australian aborigines would have noticed."

"In rural areas in France people take the existence of witchcraft for granted to this day," Alex replied with amusement. "A few years ago my sister sent me a book by a French ethnographer about witchcraft in the Bocage, in Normandy. I don't know why she sent it, but it was fascinating. The woman who did the study was convinced that some people really did suffer unlikely strings of misfortunes, including sickness and death.

"Her study had something in common with the one you read about," he said to Akiva. "Although people were sure they were bewitched, they could only make wild guesses as to how it had been done. They would suggest that an illiterate neighbor had done it by reading magic spells out of an evil book passed down to him by his equally illiterate parents. And she never found anyone who claimed to have bewitched someone else, though there were people who supposedly were able to counteract a spell by turning it back on the original witch."

"So you believe French peasants go around bewitching each other?" Mina asked Alex incredulously.

He shook his head. "No. I said that it convinced her, not that it convinced me. What impressed me was the intensity of the hatred so many of the people felt for their neighbors and relatives. It would be convenient to believe that has no effect, with or without a conscious wish, but I'm not convinced of that either."

Alex hadn't been accurate when he said that he didn't know why his sister had sent him that book; she had sent it because Sylvie, his oldest and closest friend in Paris, had given it to her to include with some others she was about to mail. What he didn't know was why Sylvie had wanted him to read that particular book. Every once in a while she would send him a book, a record, or a clipping that she thought might interest him, perhaps just to show that she hadn't forgotten him.

Alex had met Sylvie on his first day at school. The other pupils had not known what to make of him, since he spoke unaccented Parisian French but seemed to be unfamiliar with the current slang. On the first day of math class, however, he won a place in their collective memory by becoming the first student whom the instructor, an unpopular martinet who had terrorized generations of students, hadn't been able to embarrass. The incident occurred when the instructor stopped in the middle of a complicated disquisition on the course material to make an example of Alex for looking out the window.

"Am I to understand that you find the scenery more interesting than what I am trying to teach you?" he asked ominously.

"No, sir," Alex answered politely. "It's just that the scenery is new to me, but I've already learned about functions."

"Oh, you have, have you," the professor said with quiet anger, and proceeded to quiz the cheeky pupil on the most complicated examples of all the types of problems they would learn to solve during the semester. As soon as he realized that Alex did actually know the course material his manner changed.

"You're quite right," he said calmly. "There has obviously been some mistake, and you're in the wrong class. Please come to my office later and we'll straighten it out."

When Alex found the office, Sylvie was already waiting there to see the professor. She also knew that she was in the wrong class, but for the opposite reason. She had chosen literature as her major subject, and after the first day of this class already knew that it had been a terrible mistake to let them put her in a program that included any math class, even this one for humanities students.

Her interview with the professor went badly. Her plea of being totally unsuited for any math course was not accepted, and she left his office feeling miserable as she realized the extent of the disaster.

Alex, on the other hand, succeeded in arranging things with surprising ease. The instructor had already verified that he had registered as a math and science student, and he would be transferred to the appropriate courses immediately. He left the office cheerful at the unexpectedly quick resolution of a bureaucratic problem, only to stop short at the sight of Sylvie sitting on the bench in the hallway and crying.

"What's the matter?" he asked her. She only sobbed helplessly in answer to his question, so he squatted on his heels in front of her and asked again. He obviously wasn't going away, so she controlled her crying as well as she could to explain that the professor wouldn't let her leave the course. His bewildered expression made her angry.

"Oh! What do you know about it?" she said impatiently. "I won't be able to understand anything in that class! Not anything! It's always the same, I try and try, but I can't do it! This class will ruin the whole year, and in the end I'll flunk anyway!"

"It can't be all that bad," he tried to tell her, but he was only making her more unhappy.

"You don't understand," she said miserably. "You just don't understand."

"I understand that you can do this math if you want to," he said resolutely, holding her wide, dark eyes with his clear blue ones. "I can explain it to you."

"No, you can't," she assured him. "It won't help."

"It will," he said. "I'll explain it as many times as you need, and I promise you'll pass the course."

Sylvie had always suffered from feelings of inferiority in math and science classes, but Alex helped her to get over them. He didn't lose patience, or indicate in any way that he thought she was stupid, and maybe she wasn't, since when he explained things she could usually understand them. He promised her that she would pass the course, and she did.

The evening before an important exam he came through a snowstorm to her parents' apartment to coach her. His face was flushed, from the cold air, she thought, and when she offered to make coffee he asked for tea instead, which was unusual. It was when she handed him his cup and their hands touched that she realized that he had fever.

"You're burning up!" she said. "What are you doing here? You should be home in bed!"

"I promised you that you would pass this course, and I intend to make sure that you do," he answered.

"At least you could have told me to come to you," she scolded him, conscience-stricken.

"If I had done that," he replied, "you would have known I was sick, and with that excuse you wouldn't have come at all."

In return for his assistance in math Sylvie offered to help him make up the material he was missing in French literature and history. He accepted politely, but it quickly became clear to her that he didn't need her help. He read the material on his own and remembered everything that needed to be remembered.

There were two things she was able to do for him. One was to show him her Paris, all her favorite places in the city that had always been her home. The other was to read French poetry to him. He was happy to listen to her for as long as she was willing to read, and he told her that the words on the page meant nothing to him; they became beautiful only when she read them.

Except for the ritual pecks on the cheek, he only kissed her once, toward the end of the school year when they were both almost seventeen. She took him to a friend's eighteenth birthday party and they drank champagne, which neither of them was used to. It was late at night when he sat beside her, one arm carelessly resting of the back of the couch above her head, and half turning toward her and dropping his arm to hold her in a one-armed embrace, kissed her thoroughly on the lips.

She was suffused by warmth and feelings of trust and—had it been love, after all? She had wondered sometimes afterward, when she was caught up in the turbulent, painful relationship with the man she later married and divorced. At the time, she felt it to be a fierce protectiveness for the boy who had such a generous spirit and was so careless of himself.

She was suddenly frightened for him, that in spite of and even partly because of his abilities so freely shared, he wouldn't be able to get along in a harsh world without someone to take care of him. When he falls in love, the woman had better be good to him, because if she hurts him, sweet and gentle Sylvie found herself thinking, I'll track her to the ends of the earth and kill her!

The following year they had seen less of each other. She had met her future husband and Alex had made other friends, both at school and at the bookstore where he worked. Now they met only rarely, when Alex went to Paris to visit his family.

CHAPTER 6

Sunday morning Alex went into Ilan Falk's lab to tell Rafi that he had just mailed the letter of recommendation. The mess from the gas explosion had been cleaned up, and everyone was hard at work, probably more calmly and efficiently than if Ilan had been there. Shosh was wearing a white lab coat over her jeans and sweater. She looked up from her work to give him a quick smile, and all at once the day seemed sunnier.

Alex also wanted to ask Rafi some questions that hadn't occurred to him in the immediate aftermath of Ilan's death, but which now seemed important. "About the explosion, Rafi," he said, speaking quietly to avoid reminding Shosh of the subject. "Do you know whether it was Ilan himself who turned the gas on that day?"

The police had seen no reason to investigate Ilan's death. They assumed that it was an unfortunate lab accident, and at first, it hadn't occurred either to Alex or to anyone else to disagree with their conclusion. Once an alternative possibility came to mind, however, it was obvious how appallingly simple it would have been to arrange such an "accident." Alex hoped that someone in Ilan's group might have left the gas on, so that he could put the matter out of his mind.

"We've gone over that thoroughly among ourselves," Rafi assured him, "and we're pretty sure it was his own fault. Neither Shosh nor I were here at all on the day it happened—she was on vacation in Eilat, and I spent the whole day in the library. Ilan's son wasn't around either. He had disappeared without telling anyone. That leaves Kobi and Helena, and neither of them had used the bunsen burners that day. And anyway," he added conclusively, "with all due respect to the departed, the most likely person in the group to forget the gas was Ilan."

Micky stuck his head into Alex's lab during the course of the morning. "What's new?" he asked. Seeing that Alex was alone, he added, "Any more attacks by the kamikaze pilot?"

"I asked Rafi whether they had any idea who might have left the gas on," Alex reported. "Apparently no one who was supposed to be in the lab that day needed to use gas. So there are two possibilities; either it was an accident caused by Ilan himself—or it was done deliberately, possibly by someone who wasn't supposed to be in the lab that day."

"Let's look at the probabilities," Micky said briskly. "Granted, Ilan's removal was convenient for an inordinate number of people, including you. Nevertheless, no normal person had sufficient reason to murder him."

"What about his son?" Alex asked.

"I can't believe that his son would kill him," Micky replied. "I knew Ilan for a long time. He was a teaching assistant at the Technion when I was a student. He could be a bastard, but I don't think he really would have given his son a criminal record, or that Oded would have believed his threats. You don't really think it's likely, do you?"

Alex shrugged. "You knew him much better than I did." It was true that it was hard to imagine Oded Falk as a murderer, let alone a patricide. He was a thin, mousy-looking boy with a shy, self-effacing manner. It was also hard to picture him standing up to his father and driving off in the family car, but he had apparently done it never-theless. Alex had never to his knowledge met a murderer, and he had no idea how they were expected to look.

"It would be nice to know that Oded was somewhere else on the evening of March fourth," he concluded.

"In my opinion, only one of the possibilities is crazy enough to have done it, as he proved by trying to run you down," Micky argued. "And he also had the strongest mo-tive."

"Assuming that he knew about the letters Ilan was going to send," Alex reminded him.

Micky nodded. "An accusation like that would be hard to live down, even if it wasn't true. People would remem-ber that he'd been accused of faking his results, but they wouldn't necessarily hear about it or remember that he was eventually found innocent."

"Are you sure that he is innocent?" Alex asked.

Elisha had won the prize for his role in the isolation and purification of a protein factor that stimulated the produc-tion of red blood cells.

"I bet he's innocent," Micky said. "How would you fake something like that?"

★   ★   ★

Alex had stopped in at the lab for a few minutes the previous afternoon, on the way home from Yehudit and Akiva's, to innoculate a bacterial culture for a third attempt at preparing the plasmid. He had centrifuged the cultures in the morning and begun the preparation, and Arik came in after his last class to finish the procedure: Alex had to be at Daniel's school at four to see a performance by his son's class.

"How's it going?" Arik asked as he came in and took off his jacket. "Do you think we'll get something this time?"

"I don't know," Alex replied. "I made up fresh solutions and kept the samples frozen longer. But I don't think we're doing anything wrong in the isolation procedure. I've had very good results in the past doing it exactly this way. The problem is more likely to be the stage of the culture at harvest. There may be a small time window that's optimal, and we haven't found it.

"In any case, from now on, I want to save whatever we get. If we get lucky and get a lot from a single preparation that will be nice; if not, we'll pool all the little bits and go on to the next stage." By the time he finished speaking he had his jacket on and was out the door.

Daniel had one of the bigger parts in the play. A white surgical-cotton beard had been stuck to his chin and a large towel served as the long robe he wore as the pious Mordechai, whose ward Esther was chosen by the King of Susa to be the new queen. Alex appreciated the good sense of the teacher who had arranged the performance of this historical drama, the explanation of the coming holiday. She had made it short and simple, so that the cast of third-graders did it well and the audience of relatives didn't have time to become bored.

Daniel said his lines loudly and clearly, with no mistakes. The boy who played the villain had a juicier part than Daniel's and milked it with gusto, but the fair-haired, blue-eyed Daniel looked so angelic that it was clear why he had been given the part of the good guy.

At times like this Alex would think how strange it was that he should have a son who spoke Hebrew perfectly, but could speak neither Hungarian nor French. He would have to make a serious effort to teach Daniel French, he thought, so that he could communicate with his French grandmother.

Alex stayed to congratulate the teacher and say hello to some of the other parents. There were more mothers than fathers present, but he couldn't blame Varda for not wanting to come—these occasions weren't always enjoyable. Nevertheless, he almost always came, while she never did.

Alex and Daniel entered the apartment to be greeted by the savory smell of hot tomato sauce. Varda didn't like to waste her time cooking when she could be painting or socializing, but she had compromised by developing a repertoire of dishes that were both easily prepared and tasty, like this evening's shakshouka, a dish of eggs poached in tomato sauce with onion and green pepper.

She would have been happy for Alex to take on the cooking but had realized that this chore couldn't be shifted to him on a regular basis. He usually came home too late, and on days when she had become too involved in her work to prepare a dinner, he would simply put together a meal of bread, cheese, and whatever else was handy, and ask whether anyone wanted to join him.

It wasn't that he didn't know how to cook; he didn't mind making dinner on those Saturdays when the weather prevented him from being outdoors with Daniel. As a chemist, he was used to following recipes.

Daniel had the same infuriating self-sufficiency. Varda worked in a one-room apartment in a neighboring building that she used as a studio. It had whitewashed walls and good lighting, and a large part of her earnings from commercial assignments and the occasional sale of a painting went toward paying the rent. Daniel would come in during the afternoon and ask what she was making for dinner. If she said she had no time to worry about it, he would go home and help himself to whatever he could find, which was often a box of cookies. After that it would be impossible to feed him dinner. He had a nourishing meal at noon, though, at the home of their neighbor across the hall. She had three small children who needed lunch and spent her mornings cooking.

The neighbor had fallen in love with one of Varda's paintings, one that Varda was reluctant to part with. They had finally agreed that Varda would give her the painting, and in return she would give Daniel lunch together with her children. Varda had warned her that she was making a mistake; she wouldn't be able to hang the painting in her living room.

"Why not?" the woman had asked.

Varda had been unable to explain but was quickly proven

right. The bold, almost wild painting sat in the fussy little room like an eagle in a chicken coop, and the neighbor became disatisfied with her curtains. Or perhaps it was the carpet that needed to be changed, or the couch that should be re-covered.

While they were eating, Varda chatted about the work she was doing. It was more a construction than a painting, she said, but she couldn't describe it in words. So her conversation was mostly about the enthusiasm her friend Gila had shown about it.

Alex was sure the painting would be well worth seeing, since it wasn't necessary to be an art expert to recognize that Varda had great talent. But he couldn't understand why Gila's approval should be of any interest to her; Gila was one of many of her friends who seemed to have no talent whatsoever, except for self-advertisement. She was also the most irritating of the entire group, a loud woman with unkempt bleached hair, a big bust, and lots of teeth. Her idea of conversation with a man seemed to be confined to heavy flirting. Perhaps when she was alone with Varda she was able to say something intelligent.

While Alex was tucking Daniel into bed, he said, "I have to do something about teaching you French. Why don't we ever get around to it? Maybe I should find someone else to be your tutor."

"I don't like French!" Daniel replied with eight-year-old finality.

His father was genuinely upset. "But how will you speak to your family in France?" he asked.

"Why can't I learn Hungarian instead?" Daniel offered.

"I like Hungarian. I like the way it sounds when you and Aunt Eva speak it. Not the way Mrs. Kassover at the grocery store speaks it. She sounds like a duck quacking!"

"Hungarian! But that will be much harder, and also not much use. My mother can speak Hungarian, but she doesn't like it, and the other relatives in France who don't know English don't know Hungarian either. And French is much more useful in general. No one in the world except a few Hungarians speaks Hungarian."

"But you like it, don't you?"

"I love it, but I grew up with it."

"Hungarian or nothing!" the boy insisted, sensing imminent victory.

"All right, here we go. Say *Jó napot*. That's 'hello.' "

"*Jó napot*," Daniel repeated dutifully.

"*Jó napot, Eva neni*. That's 'Hello, Aunt Eva.' "

"*Jó napot, Eva neni*. This is fun! You can teach me one sentence every night when I go to bed."

"All right. Now I'll teach you one more sentence as a special treat in honor of your first lesson. *Jó ejszakát*. That's 'good night.' "

"*Jó ejszakát*," Daniel repeated exactly. "*Jó ejszakát*." *Jó napot, Eva neni*. Daddy, why doesn't Mommy learn French or Hungarian to speak to the family?"

"It's harder for some people to learn languages than for others," Alex explained.

"It's hard for Mommy to learn languages," Daniel agreed. "She didn't even learn English well. Not like you and me."

"It's not exactly the same," Alex chided. "You went to

school in America, and I had to read a lot of English when I was a student. Mommy didn't have all that practice."

"I speak English just like an American, don't I?"

"You sound just like an American to me, but you probably don't know as many words as an American boy your age."

"You sound almost like an American," Daniel told his father comfortingly. "Not like Mommy. But she could try to learn French or Hungarian, if she wanted to."

"Yes, I suppose she could."

"And she could come to my school sometimes. Why doesn't she ever come? She's not more busy than you are, and you come."

There was a silence while Alex tried to think of a suitable reply.

"Doesn't she love me?" Daniel asked.

"Of course she loves you!" Alex told him.

"I guess she loves me," Daniel agreed doubtfully. "It's just that you never know if she'll be there when you need her. Have you noticed that, too, Daddy?"

Alex hesitated momentarily, but answered, "Yes." He wasn't about to teach his son to disregard the evidence of his senses, but he hoped and wanted to believe that Varda would never be as conspicuously absent for Daniel as she had been for him.

"But you'll always be there when I need you, won't you, Daddy?"

"Yes, of course. Always."

"Good. *Jó ejszakát*, Daddy."

★   ★   ★

At nine o'clock Alex turned on the television in the living room to watch the news. The room was another, minor, credit to Varda's artistic talent. She had chosen the furnishings with great care on a small budget, and the result, in an unusual color scheme of black, white, beige, and brown, was both warm and restful.

"I'm glad the bruises on your face are going away," Varda said as she came to sit beside him. "You should be more careful where you walk."

"Yes," he said mechanically.

"Your face is what I married you for, you know," she confided. She sounded perfectly serious.

"I'm glad you told me," he replied. "I've wondered about that." For all he knew she could really have done such a thing. Although only a few years before the idea would have appalled him and even now it caused a slight cold shock, it hardly seemed to matter anymore why she had married him; whatever the reason had been, it hadn't been the right one.

All his muscles tensed as she snuggled beside him and put her head on his shoulder. He realized with a sinking feeling that she wanted him to make love to her. Obliging and not obliging were equally impossible. Why did popular wisdom insist that a woman couldn't enjoy sex without love? Varda certainly didn't love him, but she wanted to go to bed with him. What idiot was responsible for the myth that a man could completely separate his actions from his emotions?

In the bedroom, when he took off his shirt, she came and enfolded him in her bare arms, laying her head on his shoulder and pressing her firm white breasts to his chest.

Almost against his will, his own arms rose to hold her as she moved her body slowly against his, caressing his back and brushing the hollow of his throat with her lips. Breathing shallowly through parted lips, she gently traced the scars that crisscrossed the right side of his chest like the map of some nightmare country.

What sort of perversion could cause her to derive erotic stimulation from these now meaningless relics? The injuries that caused them had been of no interest to her when he was near dying of them. Taking a deep breath, he removed her hands from himself and returned them gently but firmly to her sides. Then he went into the living room to read until she went to sleep. Her attentions to these scars affected him like a plunge into icy water. Varda in a seductive mood had always been able to make him forget almost anything; almost anything, but not that.

CHAPTER 7

At the lab the following morning, Alex and Arik were gratified to see a healthy band of plasmid DNA on the minigel. "It was my magic touch," Arik boasted.

"As Otto Warburg said when he poured his rival's life's work out on the floor, if it isn't an artifact, you can do it again. Let's freeze this while we do some more preps to build up a stock, so we won't have to go back to it later. I hope nothing like that will happen again, but remember how much DNA we ran through trying to restrict with Bam HI, until we realized that it didn't cut!"

Alex was referring to a specific restriction enzyme, an enzyme that makes cuts in a DNA chain only in places where the links are arranged in a specific order. These enzymes were extracted from bacteria and named for the organism they came from, such as the enzyme Eco RI from E. coli, or Bam HI from B. amyloliquefacians.

It was a great relief to see that the plasmid preps weren't hopeless. After delivering his lecture he went back to his office to plan the next part of the cloning experiment, and also to look over the material he needed for his talk in Athens. He had to decide which slides he would need well in advance, so there would be time to make new ones if necessary.

There was one slide that he would have liked to have but didn't, because he had never done the experiment. He decided to do it right away. He happened to have all the necessary materials at hand, and if he stayed a little later and set it up, he would have the results by the end of the next day.

He had finished the work and was sitting at the desk in the lab, writing down exactly what he had done, when an alarm went off. The sudden loud noise in the silent laboratory brought to mind the recent explosion and its dread consequence. The mental image was immediately banished. This was merely the Revco, out of order again.

The Revco was an industrial-size minus-seventy-degree-Centigrade freezer. It stood against the wall in the hallway, for want of a better place, and was used by everyone on the floor to hold their most precious perishables. That included stocks of bacterial strains, expensive enzymes and antigens, and purified DNA or proteins, things that had cost a lot of money or taken much time and effort to prepare. Whenever the temperature rose above minus sixty, a loud buzzer went off. Then the repair service had to be called and all those precious materials had to be temporarily stored in another freezer.

Alex put down his pen and went out into the deserted corridor to look at the Revco. It was closed properly and all the settings seemed to be correct, so it was some sort of malfunction. Nahum Bron came up behind him. He had been in his office, working on the book he was writing. Nahum, like most professors of his age, didn't do experiments himself anymore. This often worked like the Peter

Principle: A talented experimentalist would be promoted to a position in which he was in charge of a large group of people and never did experiments himself. Nahum must have realized that managing people wasn't his strong point. He worked on an arcane subject, with only a small research group, and spent much of his time writing monographs and textbooks.

"Why doesn't this damn thing ever stop working in the daytime?" he asked testily, eying the horizontal white bulk of the old freezer. "There's a proper time for everything. The proper time for the Revco to go on strike is during office hours, when the repairman is available and there are people around to take care of it."

Alex reminded him of an inconvenient fact. "There are people around to take care of it now."

"The problem isn't moving all the stuff," Nahum grumbled, reminding them both of another inconvenient fact. "It's finding somewhere to put it."

"There's a deep freeze in the basement. There used to be some room there," Alex said. "I'll go and see." He took a moment to find the button that turned off the buzzing alarm, then headed for the stairs.

"I'll try to reach our department secretary," Nahum offered. "She may know where there's space available."

There was very little space left in the minus-seventy-degree freezer in the basement, but luckily Nahum was able to reach the secretary by phone. She told them that there were two other freezers in the building where people had found some space in previous emergencies. They equipped themselves with thick gray insulating gloves and a small metal trolley from Alex's lab, and began methodically removing boxes from the malfunctioning Revco and transferring them to the other freezers. They had to rearrange the contents of all three freezers to do it, but they managed to fit everything in.

"My hands are frozen," Nahum said when they had finished the chore, "even with these gloves. Yours must be, too. I can offer you a cup of hot tea."

Tea wasn't a drink that normally appealed to Alex, but on this occasion the fact that it would be hot was more important. He followed Nahum to his office. It was identical to Alex's, but a little differently arranged. Here an electric kettle sat on top of the cabinet under the window. There was also a tray holding mugs, a teaspoon, a package of teabags, and sugar in an empty jam jar.

Nahum handed Alex a mug of strong tea with sugar and sat down at his desk while Alex settled in one of the two chairs. "You see?" he said. "All the comforts of home."

"It feels good," Alex said, warming his numb fingers on the hot mug.

Nahum looked at Alex over the rim of his mug. "You seem to be making a habit of being on hand for late night emergencies."

"This wasn't much of an emergency," Alex replied. "Actually, the other wasn't an emergency at all. There was nothing urgent to be done."

"No, not an emergency. Just very sad. Ilan wasn't a pleasant man, but even he deserves a little respect when he's just been buried."

Nahum had been stirring his tea with angry energy. He

stopped abruptly and looked up at Alex. "Of course, you don't know what I'm talking about. It's not really important. Elisha made some vulgar remarks to me about Ilan the other day. For some reason, it upset me."

"Elisha makes a lot of vulgar remarks," Alex said.

"I know. And he was always sure that Ilan was prejudiced against him. That still is no excuse."

"Why should Ilan have been prejudiced against him?" Alex asked.

"Because Elisha's mother was Iraqi. That doesn't mean anything to me, and I don't suppose it means anything to you. For all I know, it didn't mean anything to Ilan, either. But Elisha is always ready to believe that people are looking down on him. I don't know why, it's not as if his mother had been a Kurd!" Nahum added with a bark of laughter.

It was an old joke to deflect a question by saying, "Don't ask me, I'm a Kurd!" The idea was that a Kurd was resigned to never understanding anything. There was some sort of hierarchy among the Jews from Arab countries and their descendants. It originated from the circumstances of a previous generation, when the Jews leaving those countries, often escaping with nothing but the clothes on their backs, were mostly uneducated people whose cultural background wasn't understood by the Jews of European background who received them.

Fifty years later, everyone had gone to school together, and served in the army together, and the distinction had largely disappeared. The hierarchy was preserved mainly in the minds of the people who remembered, or whose parents remembered, being snubbed or mistreated. Elisha's stubborn attachment to the idea that he was discriminated against seemed to bemuse Nahum. The whole subject was meaningless to someone like Alex, who hadn't grown up with it.

"I met his mother once, by the way," Nahum reminisced. "I knew his father slightly, and he invited me to his home a few times. We both used to study Esperanto. Did you ever study Esperanto?"

"No. Are you still interested in it?"

"I haven't done anything with it in years. It seems to have gone out of fashion altogether. A pity. It was such a good idea."

"We have English instead."

"Yes, but English is a relatively complex language, and it belongs to a specific culture. Esperanto is very easy to learn, and belongs to everyone equally."

"I never thought of learning Esperanto, but in principle I prefer to invest the effort in learning a real language. The culture that comes with it is what makes it interesting."

"Esperanto *is* a real language! But I don't want to fight with you about Esperanto, the language of universal brotherhood. What was I saying, when you distracted me with all those questions about Esperanto?"

"You were telling me about Elisha's mother."

"Yes. She seemed like a very nice woman. Nice looking too, if you can believe it."

"Did Ilan even know that Elisha's mother was Iraqi?" Alex asked.

Nahum shrugged. "He may have. They were both in the department for a long time. I'm sure Elisha thought he did."

"How did they get along together, in general?" Alex couldn't help asking.

Nahum snorted. "Just as you'd expect! Ilan was always criticizing, and Elisha is always looking for insults. I recall a few particularly unpleasant exchanges, after Ilan complained about Elisha's foul language."

"I doubt that Elisha learned his favorite Arabic expressions from his mother," Alex remarked.

The Revco repairman appeared during the course of the following morning. The compressor had failed. There was much consultation in the hallway and in the departmental secretary's office about the relative costs of replacing it and of buying a new freezer. Alex ducked out of it. He thought that he had already contributed his share of time to the latest Revco problem.

Micky caught up with him as he was leaving the building in the evening. "It's only me. Don't run into any walls," Micky admonished as he put his hand on Alex's shoulder. "I told Adi about this business," he continued. "She wanted to rush right over and tend your wounds. It was a week ago, I told her, and just a few scrapes and bruises, nothing Varda couldn't take care of with an artistically placed Band-aid."

Adi, Micky's wife, was a pediatrician. She was kind and intelligent, a small, soft-spoken woman with a cap of smooth dark hair and a lovely ivory complexion. Much more observant than her husband, she instinctively thought of Alex as someone who lived alone, though of course she knew he was married.

She hadn't forgotten the fall Saturday when Alex and Daniel came with them on a drive through the Jordan Valley to Sartaba, a desolate hill on which the Hasmonean king Alexander Yanai had built a fortress in the first century A.D.

They climbed to the top to see the ruins and to look out over the valley at the purple Mountains of Moab on the other side of the Jordan while they ate their sandwiches. In the days of the Second Temple great fires used to be lit on this hilltop. It served as one of a chain of signal posts that passed the word to communities as far away as Egypt and Babylon that the rabbis in Jerusalem had sighted the new moon. Micky knew these things, and he explained them to the others.

On the way back they bought the children ice cream in Jericho, and later, turning off the steep winding road to Jerusalem, stopped on a bluff overlooking the Dead Sea to make black "mud" coffee on a small camp stove. In Jerusalem they stopped first at Alex's apartment.

"I'll make coffee," Alex offered when they were inside.

"We just had coffee!" Micky objected.

"I mean real coffee," Alex said with a pitying look.

"Lovely," Adi accepted.

They were comfortably seated in the living room with their mugs of coffee when Varda came in with two friends. The woman had an impressive amount of unkempt hair of a peculiar shade of yellow. The young man had a ponytail and a ring in one ear and stayed very close to Varda.

Poor Alex! was Adi's first thought. No, poor Varda, she corrected herself. Varda kept glancing at Alex, who slouched in his chair with his legs stretched out in front of him and didn't seem to be paying much attention to her or her friends.

She's putting on a performance for him, Adi realized. But they're already married! Why is she acting like some teenage twit? She should be making sure he knows she loves him, not trying to make him jealous!

"We have to go," Adi said as soon as they had finished their coffee. "We have tickets for a concert this evening."

"We're going, too," Varda told Alex. "Why don't you come with us? We're going to have a little party at Gila's. Daniel can go to the neighbor's." She had gone to stand in front of Alex, ostentatiously allowing the foolishly smiling young man to keep holding her hand.

"No thanks," Alex said impassively. "I have work to do."

"Come on, Alex, be nice!" Gila, the blonde, said archly, trying to pull him out of his chair.

"Another time," Alex said firmly, freeing his hand.

Adi watched them leave, while she and Micky were still trying to collect their two children. Varda's behavior was bewildering. Could she really want to trade Alex for that young jackass?

Stupid woman! She kept playing these silly little games, and he got tired of it. She's lost him. Or maybe, she thought, with more prescience than she knew, she went too far one time, and did something unforgivable.

At the concert, with her hand in Micky's, her thoughts wandered back to Varda. With that red hair, and her green eyes and milky skin, she's a beautiful woman. She must have been a spectacular-looking child. And spectacularly talented, too. It wouldn't be so surprising if everyone made a great fuss over her and convinced her that she would always be loved, no matter what she did. They ruined her!

If my parents weren't such sensible people they might have done the same thing, she thought. I was a pretty child, and always at the head of my class.

As it was, the beautiful Varda seemed to have no idea how to keep a husband, while she herself had no such problem.

"Adi decided she could help us get to the bottom of this," Micky said, walking beside Alex through the parking lot.

"Why do we have to get to the bottom of it?" Alex wanted to know.

"What do you mean, 'Why do we have to get to the bottom of it!' Don't you want to know whether Elisha murdered Ilan?"

Alex shrugged. "We already know he would be quite capable of it," he said, "and that's the important thing, as far as I'm concerned. Speaking purely objectively, of course."

"No, really!" Micky remonstrated. "We can't just leave it like that. Adi has gotten some useful information. She's friendly with Sonia Bron, Nahum's wife, and Sonia often runs into Elisha's ex-wife, Miriam. Miriam's mother lives in the same building as the Brons, and Miriam is over there a lot.

"It turned out to be much easier than we had thought. Sonia simply told Miriam that she had heard rumors that there was something funny about the results that won Elisha the prize. Since everyone knows that Miriam has no use for her ex-husband, Sonia didn't have to worry that she would take offense.

"Miriam immediately asked, 'Did Ilan say something?' She didn't mention that she was the one who told Ilan about it in the first place, but she confirmed that he had discussed it with her. She also mentioned that he showed her what he was writing. She couldn't resist telling Elisha about the letter. That doesn't sound like a very smart thing to do, but he had said something particularly unpleasant. They had a violent argument about it over the phone. Luckily for her. That he wasn't there in person, I mean."

"Poor woman!" Alex exclaimed. "I should have thought of that. If Elisha did kill Ilan, she's in a dangerous position."

"Of course Elisha knows that he would be suspected if anything happened to her," Micky replied. "But if he's clever enough—and he is quite clever—he could always think up a convenient accident. Like the one that happened to Ilan."

CHAPTER 8

During the following days, Alex's thoughts kept re-turning to the subject of wish-killing. Aside from the fact that the idea was associated with images of witch-doctors and voodoo medicine, was there anything intrin-sically impossible about it?

Many people claimed to have had sudden inexplicable knowledge of something catastrophic happening to some-one else far away. At least some of those cases had been checked. There was also the famous Russian psychic, Wolf Messing. A number of witnesses had attested to the spec-tacular examples of his powers, including both knowledge of the past of complete strangers and predictions of the fu-ture. There were even some like Uri Geller, who could apparently bend spoons at a distance. If it was possible to bend a spoon, wouldn't it also be possible to affect a human body?

Shosh's conviction that she had killed Ilan was based on the kind of disorienting psychic experience that is usually mentally pigeonholed and forgotten as soon as possible, both by the person involved and by those who are told about it, simply because they have no place for it in their carefully constructed scheme of things. But Alex wasn't able to forget it. Although he couldn't explain what Shosh had described to him any better than she could herself, it went against the grain for him to reject it simply because he found it inconvenient. Ignoring Shosh's story would be like throwing out data that happened not to fit his theory.

Neither could he decide that since Shosh's story was inexplicable, she must be crazy. That would only be another way of throwing out inconvenient data. On the other hand, he couldn't accept such an incongruous bit of data without checking it. But how? It wasn't the sort of experiment that could be repeated. It seemed that the only thing he could do was think about it.

If wishes could kill, then Shosh's wouldn't be an isolated case. Other deaths and illnesses would also be the result of someone's wish. How many? Was a particular type of contact between the wisher and the victim necessary? Did the thoughts strike only at a person's weakest point, or was it possible to wish anything to befall anyone?

It was believed that people who were often ill might be victims of their own thoughts. Was it possible that at least some of them were victims of other people's thoughts? In that case, Alex decided, it's no wonder that Ilan had so many problems with his health; so many people disliked him! And I must be very well-liked, since I'm rarely sick. Except by the Syrians. They blasted me with a nasty thought, although it seemed a lot like a shell at the time.

It was easy to make the idea sound ridiculous. But suppose he wanted to investigate it anyway? He might start with the guilt complex. He was thinking of cases in which a person blames himself for the death of someone close to him, feeling responsible for the death because he wished it.

Among those who suffered from this feeling, might there be some who were really guilty, whose thoughts had caused death?

How could such people be identified? Some of them might have known of the death before it happened, or before they could have heard of it. Or they might have specified the actual means of the death. Shosh claimed to have done both.

Suppose that there was no such thing as a guilt complex, and that everyone who was convinced he had caused a death by wishing it was correct? In that case, those "complexes" would be impossible to cure. Of course, psychiatrists rarely, if ever, cured anything anyway.

If people could cause each other to fall sick or die by telepathy, would the best defense be wishing them even worse in return, like the so-called "unwitchers" in the Bocage in France? Could the body be protected by some form of mental discipline, like Yoga or Christian Science? Or perhaps no defense was possible.

When he went for coffee Thursday afternoon he had to maneuver past Nina, Elisha's technician, who was lingering in the doorway of the coffee room in animated conversation with two other people. Nina gave him a hearty "Hello! How are you?" He nodded and walked straight on to where the big electric kettle stood. He didn't want to tell her how he was, nor to hear how she was herself.

He had noticed Shosh sitting by herself in the otherwise empty room, and he waited for the chattering group in the doorway to leave so that he could talk to her. Nina looked from Shosh to Alex, dawdling with his coffee, and he saw the triumphant gleam in her eye.

The woman had a repertoire of off-key reactions. First she had enjoyed the idea that Elisha had physically hurt him, and now she assumed that she had caught him trying to hide a shameful secret. If he had wanted his conversation with Shosh to be secret he could certainly have managed to be less obvious about it. Nina had just failed his rule-of-thumb intelligence test. Everyone with a graduate degree had obviously done well at school: The less intelligent ones had jumped to the conclusion that they were much smarter than everyone around them and always would be, no matter in what surroundings they might later find themselves.

When the gossipers had gone and it was possible to talk in relative privacy, he sat down across from Shosh. "Have you thought about what I told you?" she asked quickly.

"Yes," he said. "I can't get it out of my mind. But we can't assume that it means that you killed Ilan. As you said, he was careless enough to have killed himself with no assistance at all. And there were plenty of other people who might have decided to help him along, either by wishful thinking or some more active means. Try not to worry about it."

"I wish I could do that!" she said wretchedly. "What frightens me is the possibility that if I did kill Ilan, I could do it again, to someone else."

His questioning look spurred her to continue. "You should have been a psychiatrist!" she said with a nervous laugh. "You see, Avi has been under a lot of strain lately, and sometimes he takes it out on me. I know it's really not his fault," she added quickly. "But I can't help reacting inside, even if I don't say anything. I can control my words, but I can't prevent myself from sometimes having negative thoughts!"

"Don't start believing that you're some kind of witch!" Alex said sharply. "You can see that people aren't dropping dead all around you, in spite of your occasional negative thoughts. Anyway," he continued, wanting to soften his tone, "Avi seems to be a healthy young man. He can probably withstand an unkind thought now and then."

"I'm not so sure about that," Shosh said miserably. "He has terrible asthma attacks. Sometimes I think he's going to choke to death. The worst ones are when somebody upsets him." Her sad little smile at Alex hinted that she lived in fear of upsetting her husband, lest she cause him to choke to death. Now she had the added fear that she could injure him even when she did nothing. Surely, killing somebody by the power of thought couldn't be that simple. Alex wished there were some way to settle the question of whether it was possible at all.

They woke up Saturday morning to a hushed wonderland in which the ordinary morning sounds were muffled by the fluffy white quilt of snow that had descended gently during the night.

Daniel was ecstatic, and Alex allowed him to go out to build a snowman even before breakfast. One had to exploit such opportunities quickly in this city; children knew from past disappointments that even the most convincing blanket of snow was liable to disappear in the twinkling of an eye once the sun had a chance at it.

After making Daniel put on his boots and jacket, Alex brewed coffee for himself. Saturday morning was the only time in the week when he bothered to treat himself to this luxury. He made only enough for himself because even if she weren't still asleep, Varda wouldn't drink it.

By the time he had finished the second cup and most of the weekend paper, Daniel came to call him to view the masterpiece he had sculpted with the help of the neighbor's children. It was very well done and was imaginatively accoutred with glasses, an ineptly knotted old tie (amazing that the neighbor had even had one), and a battered briefcase at one side, apparently dangling from a woolen-gloved hand. A broken black umbrella in the crook of the other arm completed the surreal Israeli version of a conservatively dressed British businessman. It lacked a bowler hat, but then there were limits to what could be found in even the most cluttered Jerusalem apartment.

"It's beautiful!" he told the children. "A real masterpiece! I've never seen a better snowman. Now, how about some breakfast, all of you?" They pulled themselves away from their handiwork with reluctance, but they were all hungry, so they followed Alex back to his apartment and hovered around him chattering excitedly while he made french toast and hot chocolate.

When they had finished eating, they wanted to take a walk through the newly whitened streets. The children put their jackets and boots back on, and Alex pulled on a thick cable-knit sweater that Yehudit had made for him. The color, air-force blue, was exactly the color of his eyes, and was very becoming to him. Varda admired the sweater, but was secretly puzzled that Yehudit had been clever enough to make such a beautiful thing. She couldn't have matched the color more perfectly herself.

Throwing a windbreaker over the sweater, Alex took the children across the hall to get permission for the walk from the parents of nine-year-old Ofer and five-year-old Anat. Chana was busy in the kitchen and her husband was sprawled on the living room couch, smoking a cigarette and desultorily watching the two-year-old play on the carpet.

As always, the sight of the powerful painting over the couch hit Alex with an almost physical shock. How could they live with it, he wondered. When he was in that room, even if it was only for a few minutes, he would find himself unconsciously turning so that the canvas was out of his field of vision. What sort of mood had Varda been in when she painted those violent lines and harsh colors? In her life, as opposed to her art, he had never witnessed the expression of such a strong emotion.

There was no problem about taking Ofer, but Chana, upon being consulted, thought that Anat was too little. She would get tired, walking in the snow. She would be cold. Anat, a life-size doll with blond curls and blue eyes, looked anxiously from face to face to learn her fate, and realized that the decision was going to be against her. The doll face instantly screwed itself into a horrible prelude to a howl, and the howl itself promptly emerged, accompanied by squirting tears.

Chana, wiping her hands on her apron, was anxious to get back to whatever she had left on the stove. She looked harried, but her husband simply looked resigned. Why fight it? Anat was obviously going to have her way in the end anyway, since she was more determined to get what she wanted than they were to prevent it.

"Let me take her," Alex suggested, helping them to exit gracefully from the impasse. "The snow isn't very deep, and if she gets tired, I can carry her."

The howl ended as abruptly as it had begun, and Anat ran to the door, where she turned and beamed a smile at everyone. Alex lowered himself to her level to pull the hood of her red jacket over her head and tie the strings under her chin, being treated all the while to the triumphant, conspiratorial gleam of the sparkling blue eyes. She knew that the two of them had outsmarted her parents.

It was only a short distance from the apartment building in Talpiot to the Hebron road. When they got there, they walked in the direction of the Old City. In the other direction the road soon left Jerusalem and led to Bethlehem, a few minutes away by car, and through the hills to Hebron, farther south. Here it was an uninteresting street and usually full of busy traffic, but today most drivers had had the sense to leave their cars at home; it took very little snow to block the streets of Jerusalem, because cars had neither chains nor snow tires, and the drivers weren't used to the slippery conditions.

A biting wind from the east chilled them as they passed Camp Allenby. There were no stone buildings there to offer protection, only the low huts of the World War I British army camp that now served as headquarters for the Jerusalem traffic police. Anat began to complain that her hands were cold, so Alex took off her mittens to rub the icy little hands between his own, but since his hands were scarcely warmer than hers, the benefit was mainly psychological.

"I have a pair of gloves somewhere," he told them, "but I can never find them. I can keep track of a lot of things," he said, "books, and papers, and dates, and test tubes, and shoes, and Daniel, but apparently the gloves are one thing too many."

"They're the straw that breaks the camel's back," Ofer contributed, to show that he got the idea.

"It's interesting that you always lose gloves, and not anything else," Daniel said seriously. "It must mean that all the other things are too important to lose. That's why you're more careful with them."

Eventually the high stone wall of the convent of the Sisters of Saint Claire replaced the camp on their right. After that came the road that ascended a mild incline for a few hundred meters to what Christian tradition calls the Hill of Evil Counsel. Viewed from the other side it was indeed a high hill, and the other part of the name was due to the legend that it was in his house on this hill that the priest Caiaphas conspired to do away with Jesus. The name hadn't deterred the British from picking the spot for the office of the High Commissioner for Palestine when they governed the country between the world wars. The U.N. also liked the location. The pleasingly proportioned building they could glimpse among the trees at the end of the road was now the United Nations Headquarters for the Middle East.

Finally Alex and the children reached the descent that led to the old quarry known as the Sultan's Pool, on the left, and the soaring cream-colored stone walls of the Old City high above on the right. Also on the left, above the Sultan's Pool, was Yehudit and Akiva's house in Yemin Moshe. In summer it was easy to remember that by following this road downhill they were literally going to hell, since the valley at the bottom was the biblical Gehenna.

At the low point of the road, just before it rose to circle the walls, they found Yekeziel Blum sitting glumly in his car, stuck on an icy patch that was out of reach of the sun's rays. The car had skidded and was now pointed directly into some snow-laden bushes that were all that separated the road from the quarry. Yekeziel sat stiffly with both hands resting on the steering wheel, staring grimly ahead as if determined to continue in the direction he was facing.

Alex put Anat down and approached the driver's window. Leaning one arm on the window edge he said, "It'll be a bumpy ride through the quarry. Are you sure you don't want to stay on the road?"

Yekeziel turned with a start, but was too happy to see Alex to notice the joke. "Alex!" he exclaimed. "What luck! Can you help me get out of here? I'm trying to get to my mother's. She's eighty years old and lives by herself, and I have to either take her home with me or make sure she has everything she needs at her place. But I got stuck here and can't move. The wheels just spin."

"You steer, I'll push," Alex instructed, and, shooing the children out of the way, he went around to the front of the car and pushed until it began to roll back into the road.

"Now step on the gas slowly," he advised. He pushed the car from behind, and Yekeziel began to accelerate slowly up the road. With a jaunty wave of the hand out the window, he was on his way.

"How about it, Anat?" Alex asked the little girl. "Is everyone going to walk up the hill under his own power?"

"I can't!" she exclaimed. "You carry me! Please, Alex," she amended, remembering her manners. "I'm asking you nicely!"

"We'll push her," Daniel suggested, "just like you pushed the car. Come on, Ofer!" In an instant the two boys were behind Anat pushing either side of her back, and it didn't take her long to decide that she didn't like it. Seeing the apprehensive look on her face, Alex rescued her and swung her back onto his shoulders.

"That works better on something with wheels," he explained to the boys. "She can't move her legs fast enough to keep up with your pushing."

It was strange to see the narrow, cobblestoned streets of the Old City carpeted with snow, and the white hillsides to the east provided an odd background for its domes and minarets. But they were too chilled by now to stand around gazing at the scenery, and instead searched out an open cafe. It was a good time for hot sahleb.

Before long they were warming their hands on cups of thick, pale pink liquid lightly powdered with cinnamon. While they sipped their drinks, they talked about the weather conditions that caused snow and why it occasionally snowed in Jerusalem, the various ways animals adapt to a cold climate, and their favorite hot drinks and how they were produced.

"Chocolate grows on trees," Ofer informed them. "That's what my dad says."

"I knew that," Daniel said. Naturally, he had taken an interest in the source of chocolate long before this.

"There are chocolate trees?" Anat asked in amazement.

"Not chocolate bars, silly! Have you ever seen a chocolate bar growing on a tree?" Ofer said scornfully.

"The chocolate you eat or drink is made from a bean that grows on a tree," Alex explained. "The cocoa tree."

"And sahleb comes from a flower," Ofer added.

"Is that right?" Daniel asked Alex.

Alex nodded. "It's made from orchid roots. The thickening is gum arabic. That comes from the acacia tree."

When they had finished their drinks Alex decided that it was time to go back, since Chana would be expecting the children for lunch. Did Varda have plans that included Daniel and himself? He didn't know. She might easily be busy with her friends and be obviously annoyed to see them return; or she might have prepared a meal and be unreasonably angry if they weren't on time to eat it.

It was a position in which he found himself fairly often, in spite of his efforts to avoid it. In order to be with Daniel, he had adjusted to the unpredictable demands of life with

Varda just as he adjusted to bad weather. He knew of no other way to deal with her. Varda was like the weather: It was possible to complain about her, but impossible to change her.

By the time they had finished their drinks, clouds had moved in to cover the sky and the temperature had gone down, so Alex asked them not to dawdle. There were few customers because of the weather, but the shops were open and the merchants had arranged intriguing displays of their wares on the streets. They hurried through the lane bordered with beads and trinkets, carpets, embroidered dresses, sheepskins, and carved trays and spouted jugs of polished brass.

In spite of his father's injunction to hurry, Daniel's eye was caught by a curved dagger in a silver case, and his exclamations drew the attention of Ofer and Alex. It was only for an instant, but that was enough time for Anat to disappear. The three of them looked up and down the street, bewildered by the speed with which she had vanished.

"Let's each take a different shop to check!" Ofer called, already on his way into the shop to the left of the one with the dagger.

"No!" Alex said quickly, "Stay out here in the street, Ofer, and watch for her. Daniel and I will check the stores."

Alex went into the store to their right, while Daniel went into the one on the left. In a moment they were both back outside. Then Daniel went to the next shop, and Alex went across the street. There a young couple stood with their heads bent over an amber necklace that lay on the glass case, watched closely by the owner of the store and with even more rapt attention by a blond, blue-eyed tot.

"Anat!" he exclaimed in relief. The young man looked up, and a comical expression of dismay spread over his face as he recognized Alex.

"Hello, Oded!" Alex said, surprised to run into Ilan's son. Oded dashed out of the store and began to run up the street, leaving a trail of footprints in the thin layer of snow.

Anat's brother appeared in the doorway. "There you are, you little brat!" he said, and in the same breath, "Alex, is that man running away from you?"

"Yes," Alex said, "but—"

"Don't worry!" Ofer shouted, already on his way, "We'll catch him for you! Come on, Daniel!"

Alex scooped Anat up in his arms, an awkward package that could say "Oof!", and hurriedly apologizing to Oded's confused friend, dashed out of the shop, and ran up the street in pursuit of the two boys.

"Daniel! Ofer! Stop!" he shouted after them, but the exertion didn't leave him much breath for shouting. If this was what happened when he tried his hand at detection, he thought, maybe he should stick to biochemistry.

It was only at the top of the gentle slope where the street ended at the entrance to the Old City that he caught up with Daniel. Ofer had run down a side street, still hoping to catch his quarry.

Alex plunked Anat down unceremoniously, receiving an infinitely hurt and reproving look. "For god's sake, Daniel!" he said, after recovering his breath. "What do you boys think you're doing?"

Daniel had the good grace to look sheepish. "Didn't you want us to catch that man?" he asked.

"No! I know him, and I would have liked to talk to him, but he doesn't have to talk to me if he doesn't want to."

Ofer soon returned, fortunately having lost the trail, and after Alex had settled Anat on his shoulders, they walked home as quickly as possible on the icy snow.

Chana had characteristically prepared an abundant meal that today included vegetable soup and roast chicken. "Thank you very much for taking them out," she said to Alex when they returned. "I hope Anat wasn't too much trouble."

"She was no trouble at all," Alex assured her. "I enjoyed her company."

"Please stay for lunch," Chana pressed. "I'll run over and invite Varda. As usual, I made enough food for an army, and we all want you to stay, don't we, Anat?"

The little girl reflected seriously. "I want Alex to stay all the time," she decided. "Daniel can stay, too, if he wants."

CHAPTER 9

The day after the snowy Saturday when he had un-willingly chased Oded Falk through the bazaar, Alex received a letter from his sister in Paris.

"Sylvie came with mother and Grisha to see the perfor-mance at the Opera last night," she wrote, "and we had a little party in my dressing room afterward. She's doing very well running a business, in spite of having been so bad at math in high school." Sylvie, who was tall, slender, and beautiful, had worked as a model while she studied French literature at the university, and she had later opened her own boutique.

She wasn't so bad at math, Alex thought. He recalled their first meeting, when he had offered to coach her. He had been sure that she could pass the course, because from the few sentences they had exchanged before she went in for her interview with the professor it was clear that she was no fool. He thought that any normal person could learn math, although some people were irrationally prejudiced against it.

As it turned out, his impulse to help her had changed his life much more than hers. She had only passed a math course, but he had met someone unique and wonderful. She made his life better even from a distance. It was a black depression that wasn't lightened by the thought of her smiling face.

She had another look that it didn't help to remember, one that could make a man melt into his shoes. Fortunately for his peace of mind, she had turned off that look when she got married. Had she turned it on again after her divorce? Not for him, at any rate.

He remembered the long walks they had taken on Sundays when Sylvie was introducing him to Paris. Once they had spent hours rummaging through the booksellers' stalls along the Seine, and Alex had been so fascinated by the curious old volumes that it took him a long time to realize that Sylvie was no longer at his side. Looking around, he saw that she had seated herself on the low cement embankment and taken one shoe off to inspect her chafed and bleeding foot.

"I thought these were comfortable shoes," she said as Alex approached, "but I guess they're not good for so much walking."

"We should have stopped walking long ago," Alex reproached her, "before it got rubbed so raw."

"I know," she said, "but I didn't want to spoil your fun. You were having such a good time."

"Sylvie!" he had exclaimed. "You shouldn't do things like that for people!"

"I didn't do it for 'people,' Alex," she had retorted. "I did it for you!" The words had thrilled him, but he had made himself turn away from the expressive dark eyes looking so warmly into his own.

Even Alex, who didn't share the fondness of some of his

peers for fantasizing about what the girls of their acquaintance would do for them, couldn't help but understand long before this that there was probably nothing Sylvie wouldn't do for him. The realization forced him to maintain a consistent platonic friendliness at the cost of almost unbearable tension. He was afraid to do anything else. There was no danger threatening his sixteen-year-old life that was nearly as appalling as the very real one that an innocent girl like Sylvie, who meant so much to him, would repay him with her body for a little help in math.

During the next year Alex had become friendly with a pretty university student who came to the bookstore where he worked. She had flirted with him outrageously enough to convince him that she was attracted to him in spite of his youth, and he had enjoyed her company and her bed until she went off to look for a husband.

On Monday Oded Falk turned up at the university. He stopped short on seeing Alex coming toward him in the hallway, but it was only a momentary hesitation. "I'm sorry I ran away from you Saturday," he said as they met, looking embarrassed. "There was no reason for it. I just suddenly remembered my mother telling me that you knew about the police looking for me. It was stupid! The whole thing was over and done with, and even if it hadn't been, I wouldn't have been afraid you would turn me in, or anything. I don't know why I did it."

"That's all right," Alex said. "No harm was done. But you did leave some very surprised people behind you."

"I know!" Oded said. "My girlfriend had a lot to say about it when I got back to her place! She lives in the center of town not far from the Old City, and we had walked over from there."

"I gather that business with the police was the reason you disappeared from the lab so suddenly, just before your father died," Alex probed, not liking it but feeling that it was something that had to be gotten through, like a visit to the dentist.

"It was definitely not the time to be under my father's eye!" Oded said. "So I went to Eilat for a few days with my girlfriend and some friends of ours. It was a funny co-incidence—Shosh was there, too. We ran into each other on the beach the same evening my father died."

"It's beautiful on the beach in the evening," Alex prompted, thoroughly disgusted with himself. "Did you and Shosh get there in time to see the sunset?"

"Actually, we did," Oded said. "My friends and I watched the sunset and then stayed there until it was completely dark. It was even more beautiful after the moon rose. Shosh missed that because she and her husband were in too much of a hurry to wait. Some people don't know how to enjoy a vacation!"

Alex had been irrationally pleased when Oded seemed to confirm that Shosh had been far from Jerusalem when Ilan died. It was too bad he hadn't left it at that. Now all he knew for sure was that Shosh had been in Eilat when the sun set. Eilat was about four hours from Jerusalem by car, and less than an hour away by plane. It was after ten when Ilan died.

"Your vacation must have ended very suddenly," he said sympathetically.

Oded nodded. "At first I felt awful that Dad died mad at me," he confided. "But then I realized that he must have gotten over it by the time the accident happened. He had a short fuse, but he never stayed mad. I knew from the beginning that he would never follow through with his complaint to the police. He was really the nicest, kindest man in the world. But I don't have to tell you that. You knew him."

Afterward, Alex felt like a fool. He was looking for suspects for a murder that probably hadn't been committed, and going about it very ineffectually, to boot. He wasn't a policeman. He didn't have police methods at his disposal and had no stomach for this underhanded probing of people he knew. Worst of all, he wasn't the least bit objective. He found it easy to suspect Elisha, because he disliked him, and hard to suspect Shosh, because he would have liked to take her to bed.

She didn't have to mention her hatred of Ilan to him, he thought in her defense. He need never have had any reason at all to think of her in connection with murder.

That's true, he countered in the capacity of devil's advocate. But there must be people who know her better who knew how she felt. If finally she was driven to murder, remorse might have sent her that dream afterward, and it could be remorse for the real thing that compelled her to talk about it.

It was interesting that his mind insisted on blocking the idea that a fervent wish had the power to kill. It was easier to accept the ridiculous idea he was entertaining at that moment; that the girl had planned and executed a cold-blooded murder.

The remaining weeks before the meeting passed uneventfully. Alex saw Shosh often, either in the corridor or in the coffee room. She never failed to give him a warm smile and receive one in return. Once she told him, "You were thinking of me last night, at about ten o'clock."

He felt himself reddening. "I probably was. How did you know?"

She shrugged. "I felt it," she said.

Saturday was clear, windy, and not too cold. Varda was in a buoyant mood.

"Why don't you take Daniel out to fly his kite," she suggested to Alex, "while I make a lovely lunch."

That was such a generous offer that they were on their way within thirty seconds. Alex couldn't help wondering what had put Varda in such a good humor. It was nothing to do with her painting, or she would have told him all about it. It must be something in her private life. Given the state of the relations between them, whatever it was, it was none of his business. That was a good reason not to speculate about it. An even better one was that if he really tried he could probably figure it out.

A fifteen-minute walk brought them to the Tayelet, the promenade that followed the edge of the hillside from the Hebron Road nearly to the U.N. headquarters. From the paved walk along the top of the hill there was a stunning view of the southern walls of the Old City and within them the silver and gold domes of the two great mosques, El Aqsa and the Dome of the Rock.

Clever landscaping had turned the steep hillside all the way down to the valley below into a modern garden whose walks were bordered with beds of green and ornamental grasses, flowers, and trees. Benches and pergolas placed along the paths that wound downward through the park tempted the visitor to stop and enjoy the view. There was an outdoor cafe near the bottom and children's playgrounds. The Tayelet was a popular Saturday destination for people from all over the city. It was also the perfect place to fly a kite.

Daniel's kite displayed a picture of Superman, which wasn't appropriate, since it didn't fly very well. Luckily the wind was good, so they easily got it into the air. Daniel ran back and forth with the kite in the grassy area near the paved walk. Alex stretched out on the grass, leaning back on his elbows, and watched Daniel.

The wind suddenly failed Daniel. Superman began to lose altitude. The boy ran down a flight of stairs to a lower level, trying to keep the kite in the air until the next gust would carry it back up. When Daniel disappeared from sight, Alex got up and wandered to the edge of the grass to look down. A couple sat on a wooden bench immediately below him. The girl's honey-colored hair was tied in a ponytail. The fellow had a headful of black curls.

"We shouldn't have come here," the man complained. "The olive trees are already in bloom. The doctor said the olive trees are the worst thing for me."

"There are olive trees all over Jerusalem," Shosh's voice answered. "You can't avoid them, so you may as well get used to them. I'm sure the fresh air is good for you."

"I'm sure it's not good for me," her husband grumbled. "I don't know why we had to come."

If not exactly an argument, it was a private conversation. Alex hadn't meant to overhear it. He returned to his spot on the grass without making his presence known to Shosh and her husband.

Within a few minutes they came walking up the path. Shosh waved to Alex and started across the grass toward him. Her husband followed her, but didn't stay to chat.

"Don't be long," he wheezed. "I'll wait for you in the car with the windows closed."

"Hello, Alex," she said. "What a surprise to see you here!"

"I live nearby," he told her.

"We live on the other side of town," Shosh said, "but Avi insisted on coming here. I told him the olive trees are bad for his asthma."

"I know you worry about him," Alex said. "I'm sure he appreciates it."

People commonly provided touched-up versions of private conversations for public consumption. He wasn't going to ask his colleagues any more sly questions, and he didn't want to examine Shosh's remarks for sinister meanings.

One day Nina pushed open the door of the third-floor landing as he was taking the stairs two at a time from the floor below. Since she waited for him, he slowed his pace to hers as they continued up the stairs to the fourth floor.

She had been worried about him, she said. Scrutinizing his face, she asked solicitously whether Elisha had given him any trouble.

"I'm afraid not," he replied.

His answer left her at a loss, and he took advantage of the opportunity to make his escape.

He had seen Elisha only once, from a distance. He was plowing through the slush in the parking lot, a knitted cap with a silly pompom on his bullet head.

The conference was scheduled for Easter week, to take advantage of the semester break. Over five hundred scientists would be coming to Athens, and several hundred members of their families would accompany them. The subject, biological signal transduction, covered some of the hottest research topics of the day, including the recently discovered control of cell replication by protein phosphorylation.

This was the topic Alex was to speak on. He had submitted a report on the work he had done during his postdoctoral fellowship, and he had been invited to present it in a lecture. He was still working on the subject, but only in the time he could spare from teaching and the cloning project. The applied research was what supported the lab; it was much easier to get funding for something that might help to increase the world's food supply than for basic research.

★   ★   ★

Alex, Rafi, and Shosh were all booked into the Mitropoleos, a large, moderately priced hotel near Syntagma Square. Because of its size and the availability of public rooms on the lower floors, some of the sessions of the meeting were to be held there.

Nahum Bron had taken over the administration of Ilan's lab after his death and had decided that since Ilan had intended to present Shosh's work, she should replace him at the meeting. "I don't want to hear any more about it, young lady!" he had said in answer to her protests that she couldn't leave her husband, "The ticket has already been bought, and Ilan would certainly have wanted the work to be presented."

A young Greek who knew all three of them turned up at the hotel the evening of their arrival. Theo had spent six months in Ilan's lab during the period when Rafi had been starting his doctoral research and Alex had been finishing his. He had found their names on the list of participants, and was excited at seeing them again.

The night was mild, with a taste of spring in the air. Winter had ended earlier here than in the hills of Jerusalem. They strolled to Syntagma Square, still crowded at ten o'clock, and found places around one of the small tables set out on the pavement. They ate ice cream and sipped espresso, and amused themselves by watching the people parade by.

"Tell us about this government institute where you work now," Rafi said. "What do you do there, exactly? Are you making use of your training?"

"It's all right," Theo replied, "but not very exciting. I don't want to talk about that now. This is the beginning of my vacation! Let's talk about how all of you are coming home with me tomorrow for Easter dinner."

"Is your family in Athens too, now?" Shosh asked. "I thought your parents lived in a village somewhere."

"They do," Theo explained, "but it's not too far away. I'm going to drive down there tomorrow morning, and I'll pick you up at the Mitropoleos on my way. The meeting doesn't start until Monday, anyway. You said yourselves that you wouldn't even be here now if there was a flight tomorrow."

"Won't your mother mind?" Rafi worried.

"My mother will be thrilled," Theo promised.

"Thank you," Alex said. "It sounds great."

When Theo pulled up at the hotel in his old rattle-trap of a car Sunday morning, Shosh got into the backseat. She smiled up at Alex as she moved over to leave him room beside her. The movement pulled her light summer dress close to her body, making it outline her curves and inviting him to follow her. Then Theo said, "You can't sit there, Shosh! There are no springs in the backseat. Let Rafi sit there, and you come and sit beside me."

Alex consoled himself with the thought that it was really better this way. She was lovely, she liked him, and he was attracted to her—so it was best to stay away. It wasn't out of loyalty to Varda. It would have been ridiculous to be faithful to Varda, and he wasn't. But he intended to stay with her for Daniel's sake, so he had nothing to offer Shosh. He couldn't let himself become involved with a girl who was married and already suffered from feelings of guilt toward her husband.

The drive to Elatia took them through a verdant, beautiful landscape. Here and there along the narrow, winding road they were observed by alert little white goats who nestled in steep sloping meadows of brilliant green. Each village along the way was heralded by clouds of smoke redolent of roasting lamb. Theo would slow to a crawl and carefully maneuver the car through streets filled with rows of spits on which lambs browned over wood fires.

Elatia was no different, and as soon as they arrived, Rafi and Alex were sent to join the ranks of men tending the spits. Theo's father, a big, genial man with a luxuriant mustache, welcomed them with raki, and when the meat was done, his mother and sisters plied them with more than they could eat.

The whole village ate at tables set in the street alongside the roasting fires. There were ten at Theo's table including a harsh-faced old man, an uncle of his father's, who had recently returned to the village after many years in America.

Theo's younger sister was seated next to Shosh. "Your hair is so pretty," Elena said. "And I like your boyfriend very much. He is so nice."

Shosh saw the girl look toward Alex who was talking to Theo near the spit. "He's not my boyfriend," she said. "I'm married, but my husband isn't here."

"Good for you!" interjected a young woman who was standing behind them. "Who needs a husband to follow her all over? Better to get rid of them altogether." Her young husband was standing beside her, his arm around her waist. She looked up into his face, laughing, as she teased him.

The old man leaned toward Shosh. "What she says is bad! A woman must always stay with her husband. A woman who wants another man more than her husband— she should kill this other man before she is unfaithful to her husband."

Shosh looked so upset that Eleni put a hand on her arm. "Don't mind him," she said. "He talks like that because his own wife left him in America."

While they were eating, a troupe of gypsy entertainers came by and offered to dance for them. Theo's father agreed on a fee, and three dark, slender young men began to play clarinet, accordion, and drum while several other young men and girls, all in ordinary street clothes, joined hands in a line dance. After a few minutes, some of the neighbors left their places to join the dancers.

"Do you like this?" Theo's older sister asked, spreading her arms wide to include the sunny spring day, the heaped platters, and the joyful dancers. "This is what we call 'kayf.' "

They nodded, smiling.

"That's what we call it, too," Shosh said.

The Turks must have spread the word all around the Mediterranean. No wonder it had been so widely adopted; it was so much more expressive than saying "a good feeling."

The scientific lectures began on Monday morning. They were organized according to subject, so it was possible to remain in the same auditorium for an entire session, listening to talks related to a particular topic. It was tiring and hard on the eyes to concentrate on lectures all day, but there were compensations. One of these was the opportunity to meet people who had long been familiar, but only as names attached to journal articles.

One of these familiar names rose to lecture toward the end of Tuesday afternoon, and Alex learned that the H. Kraus whose work he admired was Professor Hildegard Kraus, a statuesque and stunning blue-eyed blonde of around forty-five. When he approached her afterward to ask some questions he also met Peter, a weedy youth with long, thin, pale hair and a mustache to match. Still involved in their discussion, they walked with him to look at Shosh's poster.

Each poster had been assigned a two-hour time slot during which the presenter was supposed to be available to answer questions about his work. The posters were the solution to the problem of more reports than could be presented in a reasonable time in the form of lectures. Those who preferred not to speak, or whose work was considered by the organizers to be of interest to only a small number of people, were asked to post their data instead.

A number of people had been interested in Shosh's poster, and she was relieved to find herself enjoying the presentation. The previous evening, when she had gone to dinner with Rafi and Alex, she had been too nervous to enjoy herself, and had returned to her room early to go over her material.

Professor Kraus and her student added their comments

to the general discussion about Shosh's work, and eventually left together with the three Israelis to find some dinner. They strolled toward the Plaka and went into a taverna, attracted by the sound of lively Greek music spilling out of its doors.

The atmosphere was cheerful, and the food simple but good; grilled meat, french-fried potatoes, and very fresh, crisp lettuce salad. A large pitcher of strong red wine was provided for each table and replaced as soon as it was emptied. In their case this happened with great frequency, thanks mainly to Peter.

They had finished eating and were sipping wine and enjoying the music and the company, when a group of young men and girls entered the dance floor. The girls wore full black skirts and white blouses, and had colorful aprons around their waists and brightly printed kerchiefs on their heads. The men wore white pants and shirts belted with broad red sashes. The young man who seemed to be the leader announced the names before the dances, each of which belonged to the tradition of one or another region of Greece.

After performing by themselves, the dancers went among the tables, cajoling members of the audience to join them. Many of the guests were willing to try their hands, or rather, their feet, but the girl who came to their table was unable to convince either Rafi or Peter to leave his seat. She was beginning to look crestfallen by the time she came to Alex, but he agreed and went to join the line.

"Hassapikos," the leader announced, and began a simple line dance. The tourists managed the relatively uncomplicated steps with varying degrees of success. Alex was something of a surprise to those who happened to notice, since he did the steps exactly as the Greeks did, and with his open-collared white shirt and tan cotton slacks he fitted almost perfectly into the line of performers.

When the music finished, the laughing guests made their way back to their tables, but the young dancer next to Alex kept a grip on his arm, signing that he should stay and try the next dance. It was a little more intricate, but Alex met the challenge easily.

"Pentozali," the leader announced immediately, and they began a complicated, energetic dance. With his eyes on the feet of the lead dancer, Alex kept up with each new variation with hardly a false step, to the amazement of his friends. After a narrow-eyed survey of the line of dancers, Professor Kraus, "Hildegard," stated the obvious. "He does it better than any of them."

"Where did he learn these Greek dances?" Shosh asked Rafi without taking her eyes off Alex.

"I have no idea," he replied. "I think he's picking it up as he goes along."

The quality they were unable to put into words was the combination of posture and controlled, effortless movement that makes it heart-lifting to watch a natural dancer, no matter what the type of dance.

The leader accompanied Alex back to the table, still trying to convince him to dance some more. "You must be a Greek!" he said, clapping him on the back. "Ordinary tourists never know these dances."

"I can't claim the honor," Alex admitted, "and I don't

know any of these dances, so I had to work hard to follow you. But I enjoyed it. Thank you for letting me try them."

"That was really very good," Peter told him, nodding with exaggerated gravity as he refilled his glass.

"We have discovered a previously unsuspected talent here!" Rafi contributed.

Alex had joined the dancers partly as a polite response to their invitation, mostly for his own amusement, and not at all as a public performance. The critical attention was beginning to make him uncomfortable.

"Maybe I should have been the dancer," he joked, "and left science to my sister."

"You're right," Hildegard decided, nodding to Rafi. "That was graceful and beautiful."

Alex flushed, not as a result of either wine or exertion, and took his seat without another word.

A heavyset American tourist from a neighboring table had good-naturedly joined the dancers at the beginning, but couldn't manage to go in the same direction as everyone else. He had soon gone back to his table, where he was greeted by his companions with loud jeers. When he saw Alex return to his place, next to Shosh, the American came over to slap him on the back and offer congratulations. He was about to rejoin his friends when Shosh turned to Alex and said, "I'm sorry, I think I was drinking from the wrong glass. This one is yours." She placed a half-full glass of red wine by his hand.

"Oh ho!" the American said. "I wouldn't take that, if I were you. That's the glass she slipped the micky in."

"The micky?" Shosh asked.

"You know," the tourist explained to Alex, "the stuff that knocks you out."

Alex took a sip from the glass and handed it back to Shosh.

"He's right," he said. "I wouldn't want to drink this."

Shosh blushed furiously. "I guess I didn't mix them up after all. I put one of those little packets of sugar into mine. I'm only used to sweet wine, the kind we drink on holidays."

"It's even worse than I suspected," the American continued, spinning out his joke. "I thought she wanted to knock you out, but now I see that she was trying to poison you!"

The performance ended, but the musicians went on playing their guitars and bouzoukis. Some of the patrons, mostly men, moved to the dance floor to gyrate in time to the slow rhythms. Although the figures of the dance were improvised they weren't random. There was a common style to their movements even though each dancer seemed to be in his own private world, swaying, turning, and sometimes dropping to the floor on one knee, as the spirit moved him. The locals were enjoying themselves in a particularly Greek way, each dancer expressing his mood and at the same time showing off for his friends, some of whom moved to the edge of the dance floor to drop onto one knee themselves and clap encouragement.

Peter had refused the invitation to dance earlier, but he suddenly decided to join the fun after all. His ungainly movements didn't at all resemble what the other dancers were doing, and even threatened several times to knock one of them over. Shosh turned to Alex to ask half-seriously if he was going to try this new kind of dance. At the same time, Rafi leaned across her to comment to Alex on Peter's strange performance. He didn't notice either of them. He and Hildegard, their heads close together, were trying to talk shop. The noise soon defeated them.

"I have my car here!" Hildegard shouted close to Alex's ear. "I drove here," she explained in a lower tone during a momentary lull, "because I want to have the car afterward. My husband is flying in to meet me, and we're going to drive home slowly and have a vacation.

"Peter and I are going to take a ride to the Peloponnese tomorrow, to see the scenery and discuss work," she continued. "Why don't you come along? There isn't much on the program to interest you." Alex liked the idea, and they agreed to start out early the next morning.

CHAPTER 10

A lex entered the lobby of the Aristoteles at seven thirty Wednesday morning, as had been agreed, to find a furious Hildegard waiting for him. Peter had been unable to get up and only mumbled incomprehensibly in response to her beating on his door.

"We'll go without him!" she told Alex tight-lipped, blue eyes flashing. Facing that icy glare, Alex was glad not to be Peter. It was strange behavior for a doctoral candidate at one of his first professional meetings, but Alex didn't expect to miss him.

As they walked to her car, he noticed the way she was dressed, in slacks and jacket of the same bright blue as her eyes and a simple white shirt with a printed red scarf at the neck. It struck him that her manner of dress must reflect a hard-won resolution of a serious problem; how does an unusually beautiful woman manage to be accepted on equal terms by male colleagues? Perhaps the brusque, no-nonsense manner wasn't completely natural, but had been developed together with the tailored style of dress to make the statement that she was neither a decoration nor a sex object, but a working scientist. The bold colors and fashionable scarf testified that nevertheless she wasn't prepared to fade into the wallpaper in order to cater to male prejudice.

Her car was a huge, yellow Mercedes sedan that she maneuvered expertly through the streets of Athens, taking them toward the Straits of Corinth and the route south. "I considered taking Peter with me on the drive from Germany," she said, "but luckily I decided I preferred to have the time to myself to think. Imagine having to suffer that young fool for three days!"

They were well on the way to Nafplio before she pulled up in front of a café. The small, bare room was almost filled with men, the older ones in dark suits over open-necked white shirts, some of the younger ones in jeans and leather jackets. Since the sun had already dispelled the early morning chill, they chose to sit at one of the little tables on the street outside.

An old man in shirtsleeves and apron came to take their order. Hildegard wanted her Turkish coffee sweet, but her attempts to explain this simple desire in either English or German seemed to cause great confusion.

"*Thio Kafethes, parakalo,*" Alex told the old waiter, "*Ena glyko, kai ena merithe,*" ordering two coffees, one sweet and one half-sweet.

"*Malista, Ne!*" The man nodded, relieved, and left.

"You *are* Greek!" Hildegard accused him.

"No," he protested, laughing. "I was in Greece once before, and a café owner taught me that."

With the arrival of the coffees she seemed to decide that enough time had been wasted on frivolity, and she began a thorough interrogation regarding Alex's recent work. He hadn't yet given his talk, which was scheduled for the last afternoon of the conference, but there wouldn't be much time left to discuss it afterward, so she wanted to do it now.

Her comments were very much to the point, which made the conversation useful both in itself and also as preparation for his lecture. By the time they had finished their coffees they had thought of several possible collaborative projects. Alex promised to send her an outline of the one they liked best as soon as he got home. This drive had been a very good idea, he realized. Since there was no one to interrupt them here and nowhere to go, an hour in a place like this was equivalent to two or three hours in Athens.

Returning to the car she asked, "Alex, would you like to take the wheel for a while?"

"With pleasure!" he said. He would have agreed in any case, because she would be doing a lot of driving before the day was over, but it was true that he would enjoy it. He had never driven such a powerful car in his life.

"Now," she said as he pulled onto the highway, turning to watch him, "let's settle the question of whether or not you are Greek!"

"If I were Greek," he told her, "I would be happy to admit it. In fact, I'm Hungarian on my father's side, and French on my mother's."

"And you really never learned Greek folk dances?"

"No. The only folk dances I ever learned were some Hungarian ones that my sister made me learn. A long time ago."

"Why would she do that?" she pressed. "You may as well tell me about it. I'm not going anywhere anyway."

"She was a ballet student at the dance academy in Budapest when I was in high school. She had a passion for Hungarian folk dances, and once they were going to let her demonstrate a few for some Russian teachers, who automatically looked down on everything Hungarian. She wanted to do some very complicated couple dances, but the student who was supposed to dance with her fell off a ladder the day before and broke his arm.

"She decided that she needed me to replace him, even though I didn't know the dances. I thought she should ask another one of her fellow students, but I couldn't convince her. She said they were all spoiled by too much ballet.

"I really didn't want to do it, though, because I had to give a report the next morning on a book I hadn't even read yet. It was by Mikszath Kalman," he digressed, "one of the best of the old Hungarian writers. He's worth reading, but I don't know whether he's been translated into English or German."

"I gather you agreed, in the end," Hildegard commented, displaying an unflattering lack of interest in classical Hungarian literature.

"Finally, when I kept refusing, she offered to bribe me with a chocolate cake. So I gave in. But it wasn't for the cake. When she offered to bake a cake I realized how desperate she was, and I felt guilty about refusing to do her this small favor."

"Well, how did it turn out?" Hildegard asked.

"Inedible! If I had thought for myself, instead of trusting blindly in promises, I would have realized that my sister had never baked a cake in her life, and there was hardly any chance she would be able to do it!"

"No, I mean the dances. And the book report," Hildegard said, amused.

"I managed to get through the dances without any fatal mistakes, mostly thanks to my sister's pushing and pulling. She did everything but kick me. I couldn't believe it when she told me afterward that no one had noticed. I stayed up all night after her coaching and finished the book. Fortunately Mikszath isn't a long-winded writer."

"How long has your father's family lived in Hungary?" Hildegard asked a little later.

"He used to claim that they arrived with Arpad and the seven chieftains; that was at the end of the ninth century. The Magyar tribes probably originally came from somewhere east of the Urals."

"And your mother's family?"

"Some branches lived at various times in Russia and in Turkey. But they've been in France for a long time."

The next question was inevitable. "Did you lose any of your relatives in the Holocaust?" Hildegard asked.

"None of my father's family, since they aren't Jewish. My mother and her immediate family were able to escape, but some of her relatives who stayed in Paris disappeared and were never seen again."

"I'm sorry," she said. "My father was in the army during the war; he served in the Afrika Korps, under Rommel."

He nodded, and the subject was closed. She had needed to know whether she was trying to make friendly conversation with someone who had reason to harbor a visceral hatred for all things German, and to make it clear that her father had not been one of those Germans who butchered Jews.

For his part, he felt no special constraints with Germans who, like Hildegard, couldn't have been more than babies in the early Forties, but he understood her need to know. What an appalling legacy of hatred the Germans of her father's generation had left to their children, he thought, and not only among the Jews. In fact, he thought, the Holocaust was only an abstraction for a Jew of his generation whose family hadn't been directly affected, but no German his age was able to escape its influence.

Around noon they stopped for something to eat, and Hildegard took over the driving again. She had determined to reach Monemvassia on the southern coast, and by two they were wandering up the winding streets of the old town.

She had brought a camera and asked to be photographed beside a domed church. The blue sea was behind and far below her, and wild poppies sprouted from the top of a stone wall nearby. A couple of French tourists timidly asking Alex for directions were so pleased to find another native French speaker that they stopped to chat and volunteered to take a photograph of Hildegard and Alex together.

Continuing upward, the steep path brought them to the ruins of the Byzantine and Venetian fortifications, where they sat on the ground to rest in the sunshine.

"This is really very nice," Hildegard declared with a

sunny smile. "Once I meet poor old Richard, I'll have to forget this kind of thing. He had a heart attack recently," she continued, a shadow passing over her face, "and I have to watch him. I can't even mention climbing up somewhere, because then he insists on doing it, and it would be very bad for him." Though trying to speak lightly, she was obviously deeply concerned about poor old Richard. This was normal, Alex reminded himself. It was Varda who was unusual.

There must be many women whose husbands had some medical problem. He knew two himself, Shosh, and now Hildegard. He was sure that unlike Varda, neither of them abandoned her husband when he needed her. It was lucky for him that he was generally healthy, because he already knew exactly how much he could count on Varda.

Why had he married her? How could he have been so stupid about something so important? Although there was nothing that could have prepared him for her ultimate betrayal, there had been at least one experience that should have warned him to draw back.

It had been while he was a twenty-year-old soldier stationed in the Sinai, a few months after meeting Varda and shortly after they had decided to marry. "Come to Jerusalem this weekend," she had pleaded over the telephone. "Please! I want to see you so much!"

Although he wanted to see her at least as much, he hadn't wanted to go, because there wasn't enough time. He was on duty Friday morning, and even with the best of luck would have barely a few hours with her before he had to start back. But she made it sound so important that he agreed to do his best. He did an extra shift of duty Thursday night in order to get off earlier on Friday, and he spent a grueling day traveling by bus and hitching rides, finally arriving at her apartment dust-covered and weary at ten o'clock Friday night.

Varda's roommate opened the door and gave him the message with obvious embarrassment. Varda had gone to a party in Tel Aviv; she would see him the following weekend.

He knew better than to marry a girl who could behave like that, no matter how beautiful, how talented, or how much she claimed to love him. But it's one thing to know something and another to accept it. It had been so hard for him to give her up that the next time they had met he had gladly allowed her to make him forget his misgivings.

"Are you married?" Hildegard asked. When he said that he was, she added, "I wonder if your wife appreciates how well off she is now, with a young, healthy husband. I hope she never has to find out how terrible it is to see a strong man lying helpless in the hospital."

It would have been hard for Alex to find a suitable reply to this, but fortunately she didn't seem to expect one. There was a long drive ahead of them, and after a few more minutes they started back down the path that led to the town and the highway.

Would Hildegard have thought him a strong man lying in the hospital? He didn't think so. Not during the initial blurred period when they had seemed to be trying doggedly to fix the unfixable in an unending nightmare of pain, drugs, and operations; nor afterward, when he had been conscious for the most part and found it no improvement.

Alex tried to avoid thinking about the time in the hospital, but too often it slipped into his thoughts, unwanted and unexpected, like a hidden infection that periodically bursts through to the surface of the body. Probably he would never be able to put it entirely out of his mind. At least, not until he was able to understand how Varda could have left him alone there like a squashed bug.

He had been trying to pull a wounded soldier to safety when a shell exploded close to his right side, shattering ribs, shredding muscles, and puncturing his right lung.

When he woke up in the hospital, he felt as if fiery pincers ripped his chest at every breath. He had tried holding his breath for a few seconds to get some relief, but when he released it he was forced to draw a deeper breath than before. The result caused an involuntary gasp that prompted the doctor to assure him that he would prescribe a pain-killer. But whatever it was that they gave him seemed to leave the pain intact, while sapping whatever strength he might have been able to muster to resist it.

"I'm sorry," the doctor had told him, standing over his bed, "but I can't give you anything stronger. You're not a terminal patient. If you survived this long, you're going to live and, we hope, go home well. In the meantime, I'm afraid we have to ask you to suffer a little in order to help us fix you up. We need to be able to get a response from you if for any reason you start to feel worse."

Alex didn't believe that it was possible to feel worse, but he knew it would be futile to expend his hard-earned breath on a metaphysical argument with the doctor. And if it was possible, what sort of response did they think they would be able to get out of him then?

He learned to take rapid, shallow breaths, which held the pain at the level of extreme, grinding misery. But when he fell asleep he would dream that he was being crushed under the treads of a tank or being dragged down to the bottom of the ocean. Then he would wake gasping for breath in a reflex that caused such agony that he could neither see nor hear, only lie rigid trying desperately to calm his breathing and waiting for the shock waves to pass. He dreaded sleep, but he couldn't avoid it any more than he could avoid breathing.

Sometimes, when he regained consciousness of his surroundings, he would realize that one of the nurses had come to hold his hand. The reminder that some of his fellow creatures wanted to help him made the pain slightly more bearable. Some of them, but not his wife.

Once he had opened his eyes to see a plump, gray-haired nurse who had reminded him of his grandmother. And several times it had been a young man. He learned afterward that the male nurses were Arabs from towns and villages in the neighboring Galilee. While almost all Jewish nurses were women, it was more often Arab men who took up the profession.

The only one of them who had spoken to him, as far as he knew, was the little apple-cheeked nurse whom he had never seen again afterward. She had been sitting beside his bed when he woke from one of the nightmares, less frequent now that he was recovering from the pneumonia that had developed in his damaged lung. She must have been squeezing his hand hard for quite a while by the time he realized that she was there. With an effort he opened his eyes to see the rosy cheeks and curly dark hair. Gradually, her voice had penetrated the perpetual fog with which they had managed to enshroud his brain.

"You're going to be all right!" she was saying urgently. "They're all finished with the operations and you're getting better. Do you understand? It will stop hurting. Soon."

Varda hadn't come until her vacation was over, even though the army had reached her before she left to tell her where he was. Even if she didn't love him, she should have come. They lived together. She was his wife and his only family in Israel. No matter what extremes of self-centeredness he had become used to during his years with her, he hadn't realized that she was indifferent to whether he lived or died.

The young apple-cheeked nurse had been right. He was much better by the time Varda appeared, her luxuriant red hair and a bright yellow blouse making her seem like a ray of sunshine.

They had promised to take out the I.V. that morning; it had been important to him. Having found neither love nor sympathy, he was strongly averse to arousing pity in his wife. But hospitals being hospitals, of course they didn't actually remove it until the next day. And Varda being Varda, of course it didn't make any difference.

He couldn't have looked more helpless when she arrived. His head was resting on the raised back of the bed and his left arm was lying awkwardly on top of the sheet, immobilized by the transfusion apparatus. Because it was difficult to maneuver a shirt over the tubes and dressings, nothing covered the torso swathed in bandages. The pallor resulting from loss of blood was compounded by weeks in the hospital.

"Oh!" she had said. "Are you all right? I hope they're taking good care of you." And had proceeded to tell him all about her trip. He hadn't had the strength to pay attention but it didn't matter, because he wasn't required to say anything. He decided that when he regained more energy it would strike him as funny, but in the meantime he had hoped she wouldn't come again.

Two weeks later the hospital was ready to send him on to a nursing home for a few more weeks of convalescence. The day before he left, the doctor who removed the bandages gave him a lecture.

"You're a young man, and you're used to the idea that you can do anything," he began, although in spite of a receding hairline he obviously wasn't much older than Alex. "You have to realize that those days are over. Several internal organs have suffered severe damage. There are lots of adhesions that could rip apart. It's all one big patch job in there," he went on as if speaking to an idiot. "So—no strenuous effort, if you don't want to find yourself back on the operating table. I can't promise, you understand, but in my opinion, if you take good care of yourself you could be all right for years. Good luck."

Alex had thanked him and the other doctors and nurses for saving his life, and promptly forgotten his advice; time enough to worry about disabilities when he ran into them. The army continued to call him for annual reserve duty, although he was no longer fit to jump. Nowadays they used him as an instructor in the training of new medics.

⋆   ⋆   ⋆

Although the convalescent home was also in the north, Varda came to see him there during the first week of his stay, this time bringing Daniel. Judging by the little boy's hysterical excitement, he might have expected never to see his father again.

Alex stood up and walked toward them as they came in, and Daniel ran to clutch his leg, begging to be picked up. He couldn't help remembering that he had hesitated, afraid to reactivate the nerve endings that had made his life not worth living for the past weeks. How long had he stood there while the frantic child looked up at him, not under- standing why his father refused to take him in his arms?

Although his worst fears weren't realized, the strain on the muscles of his chest had hurt like hell, and noticing a nurse bearing down on him with her mouth already open and the light of battle in her eye, he carefully shifted the weight to rest entirely on his left side and went to sit down with Daniel on his lap. He remained there, clinging to Alex, while Varda chattered about her various plans and activities.

"What's the matter?" she had asked eventually, noticing that he wasn't responding.

"You!" he told her. "How could you go off on vacation and leave me to live or die on my own until you got back?"

"It was selfish of me, I suppose," she admitted disarm- ingly, "but I wanted so much to go to Italy, and you know how I hate hospitals! Anyway, they told me you were unconscious. Of course, if I had known it was important to you I would have come."

"Oh, well," he had replied with complete honesty, "if you preferred to be in Italy, then I preferred for you to be there."

Daniel wouldn't let himself be taken from Alex when Varda wanted to leave. The past few months must have been traumatic for a two-year-old child, Alex realized. First his father had disappeared, then his mother, and he had been left, screaming, according to Varda's report, with a cousin of hers whom he barely knew.

As Varda pulled Daniel away, sobbing inconsolably, she promised him that Alex would be home soon. Alex knew that it was true. He had barely had time to reach the obvious conclusion, that he would have to leave Varda as soon as possible, before being made to see that he couldn't leave at all.

Hildegard was at the wheel again as they headed back north from Monemvassia, and they covered about forty kilometers in good time. At Vlahiotis, her guidebook said, there was a turnoff to a more scenic route that wouldn't add any mileage.

"Look out for a road leading off to the right," she told Alex. There was no road leading off to the right, but she was unwilling to give up the idea. She drove back past the place where the road was supposed to be.

When they passed the same stretch of highway for a third time without finding any road, she suddenly swerved the yellow Mercedes sharply to the right onto what looked for all the world like a farmer's dirt track.

"This must be it," she said.

"It doesn't look like a road," Alex protested mildly.

"Let's follow it for a while and see," she replied.

The track continued for several kilometers. Then it began a curving, bumpy descent, and it wasn't until they were near the bottom that they realized that it had come to an end.

Hildegard stopped the car at a boulder that blocked the way. There was a track winding upward on the other side of a dry stream bed, but it was impossible to get there.

They couldn't reverse the Mercedes up the steep winding track all the long way back to the top. The trail was barely as wide as the car, and the crumbling edges made it even narrower. Getting out of the car, they examined the boulder and saw that it was anchored deeply in the roadway and definitely immovable.

"Sorry," said Hildegard, looking depressed. "I suppose there's nothing we can do now except leave the car here and start walking."

"We can get the car past this," Alex decided. "The body will hang over, but there's enough room between the rock and the edge for the wheel base. The track on the other side of the riverbed should get us somewhere."

"Do you think it will pass?" she asked dubiously. "It doesn't look wide enough. I don't believe I can do it."

"I'll drive. Stand in front and direct me," he told her, getting into the driver's seat.

He released the brake and began to roll forward slowly,

concentrating on Hildegard, since he could see neither the rock nor the edge of the road under the broad vehicle. She kept her eyes on the wheels, her face set in a frown, and signaled with her hands that he should keep now a little more to the right, now to the left, toward the disintegrating edge of the track.

At the top of the bluff on the far side of the wadi they found themselves amid olive groves and meadows carpeted with wildflowers. Ahead a broad dirt road led to a town whose white houses sprawled up a hillside in the distance. That had to be Geraki. The route that had brought them there was scenic, just as the guidebook promised.

Alex drove the yellow Mercedes up onto the first paved street at the edge of the town directly out of the surrounding fields, an apparition which fortunately there were no townspeople around to see. They saw a local woman at the side of the road, a kerchief covering her head and a straw basket on her arm.

Alex stopped the car and leaning out, scraped together enough elementary Greek to ask her, "*Pou eine o megalos thromos?*"

She pointed back in the opposite direction, so he drove on a few meters and made a U-turn. When they passed the woman on their way back, another woman was standing beside her.

"How did you speak to the foreigners?" the second woman asked. "You only speak Greek!"

"I don't know. He asked, 'Where is the big road,' " he heard the first woman reply.

At the first town they came to on the highway, Hildegard said, "Stop here, please. I want to buy you a beer."

"I don't know how I agreed to let you do that!" she said when they were facing each other over two beers in a cafe. "I had your life in my hands."

"But you directed me very well, and returned my life to me in the same condition in which you found it," he replied lightly.

All at once a smile of pure pleasure lit his face as he remembered the stern, disciplined Hildegard suddenly swerving the great Mercedes straight into the wilderness, and he raised his glass to her. "May all your off-road adventures end as successfully as this one."

CHAPTER 11

It took Alex a long time to get a cup of coffee Thursday morning, so he barely reached the hall in time for the first talk. The room was almost full. He was about to take a seat in a back row when Shosh called to him to come and join her; she had saved a place for him.

He made his way through the row toward her with mixed feelings. He couldn't help being glad that she had thought of him and happy to sit beside her. Any more than he could help knowing that it was a bad idea. It required an effort of will to stay away from Shosh. He wasn't sure that he would be capable of such self-sacrificing gallantry if ever a closer relationship were to develop between them.

She welcomed him with a glowing smile that drove all thoughts of self-sacrifice out of his head, and asked him whether he had enjoyed his trip with Professor Kraus. He barely had time to say that he had before the first speaker began, and they settled back to listen. The chairs were crowded closely together, so Shosh's arm was pressed against his, reminding him of why he had thought it better not to sit there in the first place.

At the end of the last morning session he jumped up to have a word with the last speaker. Shosh followed him and lingered in the background but if she had hoped to have lunch with him she was disappointed. Hildegard was there wearing a plain white blouse and a simple straight skirt, with a bright red jacket that set off her platinum-blond hair. She and Alex went off together and were joined by two other Germans as they left the auditorium.

Apparently the two German men were acquaintances of long standing, because she told the story of their cross-country drive in the Peloponnese with gales of laughter and much humor directed against herself, occasionally express-ing herself in German for convenience. Alex, in a navy blue V-neck sweater and white shirt, may have looked like an undergraduate, but after hearing the story the men became noticeably more respectful. They seemed to have decided that he must be someone worth talking to if Hildegard had undertaken a venture into the wilderness with him.

He saw Shosh in one of the afternoon sessions but didn't try to find a place near her. Sitting next to her in the morn-ing, he had caught himself thinking that she no longer seemed to be worrying about her husband and his attacks. But that wasn't the sort of worry that disappears after being away from home for a week, no matter how much she might like him.

Shosh, Rafi, Alex, and another Israeli from the Technion went out for dinner together that evening. It should have been pleasant and relaxing to speak only Hebrew for a few hours, but the man from the Technion had just heard of Ilan's death and kept talking about it during the meal. Shosh looked more and more nervous and unhappy. After one glass of wine, Alex's head felt strangely light, and when the meal was over and the others wanted to walk for a while, he excused himself and went back to his room to bed.

Alex realized as soon as he woke from a fitful sleep that he was sick. Since it happened to him so rarely, he decided that no virus could have done this on its own. The only possible explanation was that the fellow who had sat next to him coughing and sneezing on the first day of the meeting, although a perfect stranger, had wished him ill. But whether or not the stranger had infected him with the aid of mental machinations, no applied thought on Alex's part was able to cure the result.

It was unfortunate timing since his talk was scheduled for that afternoon, and as he felt worse and worse during the course of the morning, he began to worry about the lecture. His head reeled when he stood up at the end of the morning session, and he realized that the problem wouldn't be how well he would be able to field questions, but whether or not he would be able to stand on his feet for thirty minutes.

The chairman of the afternoon session was a thick-set Dutchman, with a fringe of sandy hair around a bald pate. Alex needed to see him before the session to hand over his slides, and he tried to beg off instead.

"Impossible!" the Dutchman said, looking at him sternly over metal-rimmed glasses. "It will make a hole in the program! It's only half an hour, with the questions. So you have a little fever, so what? You're already here— You may as well give the talk. You can collapse afterward."

The phrase, "a hole in the program," echoed in Alex's mind. He pictured muddy banks bordering a small round opening in which black water swirled and surged. He was in the water to plug the hole, but the undertow was pulling him down, down to the bottom of the hole in the program. Speaker after speaker would be sucked into this hole, each clutching his notes in one hand and his slides in the other, never to emerge again.

At the bottom they would hold their own anticonference, presenting results exactly opposite to the ones reported on this side of the hole. There proteins, before dismantling themselves into constituent amino acids, would send messages via RNA for the proper assembly of genes into chromosomes. Why not? If a biochemist could do it in the laboratory, why not a much more talented living cell?

Maybe Lamarck and Lysenko were right, in that hole he was being pushed into by the implacable Van der Hoek. Maybe there was also a germ of truth in the theory in this world, not as a rule, of course, but as an exception. Half the necessary machinery was already known, after all—the reverse transcriptase that transcribed RNA into DNA.

Of course. That would be the explanation of prions, those little proteins that countered all current theory by behaving as if they were DNA. Stop it! he ordered himself. This was not the time to think about prions.

In any case, it wasn't very exciting to watch tiny prions jumping around, and still less so to observe them as they lay supine, serving as templates for reverse translation.

If he were an astronomer, then he would have a really spectacular sound-and-light show in his head. If he could have a close-up of fiery suns whirling in their galaxies as they streaked through space, or view opalescent nebulae shimmering against the velvet blackness of the void; if, for an instant, he could imagine the myriad celestial bodies exploding, coalescing, and all the while hurtling at unimaginable velocity through the utter silence of deep space, eternally faithful to a program set in motion at some instant billions of years ago—that would be worth the price of admission. If it was only going to be prions, he wanted his money back.

It was like being under the influence of a psychedelic drug, he thought with the corner of his mind that even now sat back and observed. It was very interesting, but probably not the best mental state in which to give a scientific lecture.

The talk itself wasn't the problem. He had gone over the material so many times while writing the paper that he thought he could probably present it in his sleep, or drunk, or high on LSD, for that matter. But people were bound to raise questions afterward; he would be presenting some surprising information. Answering them would require disciplined thought, not this three-ring circus.

In the meantime someone else had engaged the Dutchman in conversation, and Alex would have to stand and wait for an opening in order to argue with him. But what would he say when the chance came? Please have mercy on me and let me go? I'm definitely too sick to talk, and to hell with the hole in your program? A sentence like that should be followed by a decisive exit, but it had become urgent that he sit down, so he went back to his seat, and after what seemed to be only a few minutes, it was time to give the talk.

When he took his place at the front of the hall, he realized that his fears had been exaggerated. The lectern made it impossible to actually fall over. In every other respect, it was a disaster. There must be some circuits in the brain that are sensitive to temperature and cease to function completely in a high fever. At any rate, he heard the many questions at the end of his talk as if they came from a great distance and hardly knew what he said in response. Judging by the confused expressions on the faces of some of the questioners, he would be better off never finding out.

The surest indication that he had made a complete fool of himself was that Hildegard felt the need to come to his rescue. She stood up to make a comment that he felt she wouldn't have bothered with if he had been functioning properly, then complimented him on the work and took advantage of having the floor to add some remarks addressed to previous questioners.

"Regarding Dr. So-and-So's question," she said, "I asked you a similar question the other day, and I think the explanation you gave me then might be helpful to him also, namely—" And she proceeded to provide some of the more rational arguments that he had given on Wednesday but was incapable of producing now.

When he left the room Shosh followed him out to congratulate him. He looked at her disbelievingly, but she insisted that it had been very good, as was clear from the number of people who had asked questions or made comments. He concluded that Shosh must have given him the benefit of the doubt and assumed that it was her fault when she didn't understand one of his answers, instead of realizing that he was at the edge of delirium.

"Just tell me one thing," he said, only half joking. "Was I speaking English?"

"Of course," she answered, bewildered.

"Good," he replied, turning to leave.

"You'll come back to go to dinner with us?" she asked.

"No," he replied. "I'm going to bed. I don't feel well."

"You don't look very well," she agreed, approaching to put a gentle hand on his forehead. "And you're very hot," she said worriedly. "I'll see if I can get you a doctor."

"Please don't bother," he told her. "I'll probably be better in the morning."

"I'll bring some dinner back for you," she promised.

"No, really," he protested. "I don't want to eat anything. Thanks anyway."

Hildegard caught up with him as he leaned against one of the rectangular marble pillars in the lobby, waiting for the elevator to take him to his floor.

"What's wrong?" she asked quietly.

"Probably just flu," he replied, "but it feels like mental meltdown. I told Van der Hoek I shouldn't speak, but he didn't want a hole in the program. So—," he shrugged dejectedly but immediately saw the funny side of his own debacle.

"He had me at a disadvantage; I was in no condition to fight about it. What bad luck! Another degree or so and I could have passed out and been spared the embarrassment."

She stepped toward him and looking closely at his face, touched a cool palm to his forehead.

"Yes," she said. "I see now. You're still young enough not to look as sick as you really are. But don't worry," she added cheerfully. "It wasn't that bad. It was only shocking by contrast with the way you spoke the other day. Plenty of our colleagues are this obscure all the time."

He had to laugh at that, although it made his head hurt. "Thanks for helping me out," he said.

"Any time," she replied with a brilliant smile. "Now, I hope you're on the way to see a doctor?"

"No," he replied. "I just want to go to bed. I'll see about a doctor if I'm not better in the morning."

"I hope so," she said as the elevator door was closing on him. She would have liked to check on him in the morning, but it wouldn't be possible because she had to meet Richard at the airport.

A woman couldn't help worrying about Alex, she thought, because he seemed to be the type who didn't worry much about himself. No doubt one of those heroes like Richard, who didn't believe in doctors. Well, probably she needn't be concerned. The little Israeli girl who followed his every move with those big calf eyes would see that he got a doctor.

Alex was awakened from a heavy sleep by persistent gentle rapping on the door. It was Shosh. She had managed to find an open pharmacy and had brought some medicine.

He was having trouble waking up, and after opening the

door, went back to sit on the bed, his head in his hands. He wore only pajama pants, because he had been so hot when he went to bed. Now the room seemed to have become colder, and he got back under the covers.

"Drink some of this," she said handing him the open bottle. "The pharmacist said it would do you a lot of good."

Unlikely, he thought, but again it was too much trouble to argue so, propping himself up on one elbow, he took a healthy swig that left him gasping and coughing.

"It's pure alcohol!" he got out between coughs. "This may help me to forget I'm sick, but I don't think it's going to cure me!"

When he had caught his breath, he turned to put the bottle down and could only stare like a fool at Shosh, who was calmly removing the last of her clothes.

"Don't," he began, as she lay down beside him, but got no further. For one thing, she had pressed her lips to his, and for another, he couldn't remember why he had wanted to refuse this.

She stroked his hair and kissed his lips and eyes as he moved feverish hands and lips from silky golden hair to perfect, rosy-nippled breasts.

He must owe her an apology, he thought. He had attacked her like—like what? Like a man dying of thirst in the desert who finds a spring of pure water. Or maybe, like a drowning man clutching at a straw.

"I'm afraid I took advantage of you," she was murmuring, smoothing his tousled dark hair. "Finding you sick, and dosing you with that Greek rot-gut."

"Yes, you did," he agreed, rubbing her cheek with his. "So I wonder why I don't feel more exploited?"

When he woke up in the morning, Shosh was gone, and the fever had broken. He didn't see her in the hotel breakfast room or in the lobby either, and he began to wonder if her appearance in his room and the surrealistic lecture had both been hallucinations.

The reality of his talk was proven when several of the scientists who hadn't yet left approached him with remarks like, "I didn't quite understand something you said yesterday," or "Would you mind explaining to me what you meant by—?" In this way he learned to his embarrassment what idiocies he had perpetrated.

One especially courtly Englishman didn't quite know how to put his question. "Surely, you didn't mean," he began. "I mean to say, it isn't possible that, er—"

"I'm very sorry for causing so much confusion," Alex said. "I should either have taken an aspirin or gone to bed, or both, instead of staying at the session and talking nonsense. Please give me another chance, and I'll do my best to pull the spanner back out of the spokes."

Rafi came into the lobby to look for him later in the morning. Their return flight wasn't until late afternoon, and he wanted to wander around the city for a few hours. Shosh had left at dawn for the airport to try for an earlier flight. She had received a telegram saying that Avi had been taken to the hospital.

CHAPTER 12

Alex hadn't felt like wandering around Athens with Rafi. Although no longer burning with fever, his temperature was still high, and the germ that had coursed so violently through his blood had left him drained. During the flight he lay back in his seat with his eyes closed and tried to think only of a few hours that Shosh had been in his arms and nothing past that, because he knew that he wasn't going to like what came afterward.

Damn the man! he thought bitterly of the unfortunate Avi. Why couldn't he have stayed well?

The following morning Alex was recovered and eager to get back to work. He had to prepare his next class, and he wanted to see how Arik, his doctoral student, was doing with the plasmids and to plan a new experiment based on a suggestion from Hildegard.

In the afternoon, Micky stepped into his office for a moment to greet him. "How did it go?" he asked, referring to the talk. "Did you make a big impression?"

"It will go down in history," Alex assured him. "I'll tell you about it sometime."

"Stop in at my place on your way home?" Micky asked, already on his way out the door. "I want to talk to you. Not here."

★   ★   ★

Micky lived in a pleasant second-floor apartment on a quiet street in Bet Hakerem, just across the wadi from the university. The building was faced with the usual Jerusalem stone, almost white in this case, although the color would sometimes be pale yellow, light beige, or most beautiful of all, pale rose. Micky's building was a relatively small one of only eight apartments on four floors, and not new enough to have an elevator.

When Alex ran up the stairs at around six o'clock, Adi had just returned from her afternoon clinic and was making sandwiches for the children. In the meantime Micky put water to boil for instant coffee. They waited until Shiri and Yuval were settled in front of the TV with their sandwiches before sitting down at the kitchen table to talk.

They chatted for a few minutes, but Micky was anxious to get to the point. "Elisha had a busy week while you were gone," he announced.

Alex waited for him to continue, but he left it to Adi. "This is from Miriam, by way of Sonia Bron," she explained. "Elisha called her last Monday and told her he had just realized that he left his gun when he moved out of the house, and he wanted to come and get it. Miriam was sure that he had taken it with him, but he insisted that it was there, and that he had to get it himself. She didn't want him to come to the house, but she gave in.

"He rarely comes, you understand, and only when the children are there, but this time of course he knew that it was the school break, and they were both away on camping trips. Miriam told him to come right away and get it over with, but he wanted to put if off until that evening.

"Since he was going to show up, of course she didn't invite any friends over that evening, but in the end he didn't arrive until ten o'clock. Even if someone had dropped in earlier, they would have been gone by then. He barged in as if he still lived there, and told her to make tea. She wanted to avoid trouble, so she just made two cups of tea and sat down with him.

"Before she started to drink hers, the phone rang and she had to leave the kitchen to answer it. At the time she thought it must have been a wrong number, because there was no one on the line. Later, of course, she suspected that Elisha had asked someone to call him there at exactly that time.

"After she hung up, she went back to the table and drank the tea. She was waiting for him to look for the gun, wherever he thought it was, but he just sat there and stared at her. She said it was very strange. She lost track of time, and she could hardly keep her eyes open.

"Suddenly, the doorbell rang," Adi recounted dramatically. "She had almost fallen asleep, but that woke her up and she got up to open the door. It was her next-door neighbor. The woman saw that Miriam was out on her feet and panicked; she wanted to call a doctor, an ambulance, the police, but Elisha calmed her down and got her out of the apartment. He must have left right afterward, and Miriam woke up on the living room couch late the next morning."

Adi paused in order to heighten the effect of her next

words. "Afterward, she heard from mutual friends that Elisha had become worried that she would commit suicide. He was afraid that she would shoot herself with the gun he had inadvertently left in the house. But she had searched the whole house while she was waiting for him, just to make sure. The gun definitely wasn't there."

Alex realized that he had forgotten all about Ilan and the possibility that someone had killed him. Elisha had been the farthest person from his mind. He had certainly been thinking about Shosh, but those thoughts had nothing at all to do with murder, by wishing or otherwise.

"It's obvious, isn't it?" Micky said. "Elisha had it all set up. He picked a time when she would be by herself, and put a couple of sleeping pills in her tea. Then all he had to do was produce the gun, which I'm sure he had with him, and fake a convenient suicide."

Apparently he had been wrong to forget about Elisha. Elisha's sudden decision to do away with his ex-wife probably wasn't a coincidence. It was more likely to be related to her cooperation with Ilan in ruining his reputation, and made it seem much more likely that he had also murdered Ilan.

"Amazing luck, that the neighbor dropped in at that hour," Alex commented.

"She's Argentinian," Adi said, as if that explained everything, "and she's always doing things in the middle of the night. She was baking a cake and wanted to borrow a cup of flour."

Micky was looking at Alex, waiting for his reaction. Alex stared back for a long moment with what Micky called the "blue look," a direct, expressionless gaze that meant only that he was thinking about something, not necessarily connected with the person in front of him.

"Enough!" he said, focusing on Micky again. "Let's put an end to this."

"How?" Micky wanted to know. "Can you think of a way to prove that Elisha killed Ilan?"

"No," Alex admitted. "But I can think of a way to get around it. We can give Elisha the same reason to kill me, and be ready to catch him when he tries."

"We won't let you do that!" Adi said, appalled. "That's not a reasonable idea! You think you're unkillable!"

"I don't think that," Alex replied.

"Why you?" Micky was saying. "We can just as well get him to try to kill me."

"Stop this! Both of you!" Adi said sharply.

"It had better be me," Alex answered Micky. "For all we know, he may actually like you, and if he doesn't take the bait we might not have another chance.

"One of you will have to get word to him that I just found a copy of the letter Ilan was planning to send. It was between the pages of the manuscript of my paper, the one Ilan gave back to me. I thought ruining Elisha's academic career by accusing him of faking research results was a great idea, so I'm going to mail the letter to the administrators of the Landon Prize, and also send copies to the faculty senate and the newspapers. We'll have to provide an appropriate witness to be around as soon as he gets the information."

"Sarahle," Micky put in. "We have the perfect person. You must have heard Adi mention her, she's her best friend.

She did her army service in the military police, and she's been in the police force ever since."

"Please find out when Sarahle can do it," Alex requested of Adi. "Whenever it is," he told Micky, "you could help me by giving Elisha the idea that my power supply has been acting up, and some electrical malfunction is to be expected that evening when I start running a gel."

Monday morning, Alex found Rafi and asked whether there had been any word from Shosh. He had just spoken to her, Rafi told him. She had called to say that she wouldn't be coming back to the lab. Avi was being moved to a hospital in Tel Aviv, so she was leaving Jerusalem; she would have left within a few weeks in any case, since now that Ilan's lab was being closed down, she no longer had a job.

Seeing that her objections fell on deaf ears, Adi reluctantly agreed to do her part. They decided that she could best pass on the message about the letters, via Sonia and Miriam. She was to do this without telling them it was a sham, but ensure that Elisha received all the important details. Also, she had to contact Sarahle.

Tuesday morning Nahum Bron descended on Alex in his office like an avenging angel. "What's this nonsense I hear from my wife?" he demanded in a furious tone that was comically at odds with the carefully lowered voice.

"You're announcing plans to ruin Elisha's life and career? Are you trying to commit suicide?"

"Your saying that shows that you agree that Elisha is

dangerous. I suppose you know why we think that he may have murdered Ilan," Alex countered. Nahum did.

"I thought that if he tries to murder me with exactly the same motive it will show that we're probably right, and if we catch him in the act, he may admit the first murder also. In any case, it will be possible to prosecute him for attempted murder and get him off the streets."

Nahum was silent for a moment. "As usual, my friend," he replied more calmly, "I can't fault your reasoning. I share your devotion to truth in the abstract. And I agree that as a practical matter, we have to know whether we have a dangerous psychopath in our midst.

"But this!" Nahum's calmness had been only temporary. "This blithe risking of life and limb! This is definitely a young man's notion of what's reasonable and what isn't."

Blithe? Alex performed a rapid mental survey of possible adjectives for his attitude to the present undertaking, and confirmed that *blithe* was not among them. Apparently he wasn't as young a man as Nahum thought.

Tuesday evening Micky called to tell him that everything was ready. Long after Varda had gone to bed, he lay on the living room sofa, thinking alternately of Shosh and Elisha. He wondered why Shosh had so suddenly climbed into his bed, and whether she would ever want to see him again. Probably not, he thought with a great sense of loss. Avi's illness would make it impossible. She wasn't another Varda; if she were, he wouldn't want her.

Elisha intruded into his thoughts less in person than as an increasing nervousness now that the final act was here.

If he had guessed correctly, Elisha would try to sabotage the suspect power supply so that he would be electrocuted when he turned it on in the evening. But there were many loopholes in that plan.

Elisha was a cunning man. He was also a big one, and he had an uncontrollable temper. He might simply come up behind Alex at any time and bash him over the head. Or he might choose to stage an accident with something other than the power supply, especially if Micky wasn't able to make the suggestion convincing.

If any of those things happened, Alex thought, only a little bad luck would be required to prove what he already knew very well, that he was killable. He didn't regret having put himself in this situation, but it was just as well that he wouldn't have a long time to think about it.

He finally fell asleep on the couch and had no sense of how much time had passed before he was startled awake by an apparition at his shoulder. It was Shosh, kissing him tenderly on the cheek.

It was over in an instant. He was wide awake now. His heartbeat was as rapid as if the flesh-and-blood Shosh had jarred him out of sleep. He tried to understand what he had seen. Not a dream. He had never had a dream in which someone appeared over his head or woke him up. Was it nothing less than Shosh herself, saying good-bye?

He lay motionless, his thoughts racing. He had learned something new and entirely unexpected. This must be what thought transfer felt like, on the receiving end. This was what people meant when they said, "It was as if he was in the room with me!" or, "She was so close I could have touched her!" These sentences were cited by psychiatrists as part of the syndrome of delusional behavior, but he didn't believe that he had suddenly begun to suffer from delusions. In the light of what had just happened, he thought it more likely that psychiatrists, even in their sleep, were uniquely impervious to other people's thoughts.

Was sleep conducive to receiving such messages? Not during dreaming, perhaps, but when one's mind was as nearly blank as possible? Were the messages sent inadvertently or intentionally? Was a specific talent or skill required—was Shosh really a "witch"?

People had been catching glimpses of this phenomenon through the ages. It was hard to believe that they weren't even sure that it existed, much less could anyone explain or control it. That put it in good company. No one could explain or control gravity, either.

CHAPTER 13

Wednesday morning, as Alex began to set up his experiment, he found himself looking at everything he touched as if it might explode in his face. Elisha could easily have booby-trapped the lab during the night. The labs were locked, but the locks were simple, and there were many master keys around.

He was interrupted by a petite, olive-skinned young woman with dark eyes and black hair wound into a neat braid. Although she wasn't in uniform, her white cotton shirt looked starched, and even her jeans seemed to have been ironed. Her earrings were neat little golden loops fitted on small, well-shaped ears.

"Sarahle?" he inquired, as she hesitated at the laboratory door. He addressed her as Sarahle, the diminutive for Sarah, because that was what Micky and Adi called her. Perhaps her parents had been the first to call her that, or maybe her friends had started it because she was small. In any case that was what she was called by the people who knew her, and he would be no exception.

"And you must be Alex," she responded, coming in and offering her hand to shake.

Adi had explained the situation to her, and she in turn had discussed the matter with her supervisor and received permission to play her part. From the police point of view, there was no evidence to justify an investigation of Ilan Falk's death. However, they accepted the possibility that a murder might have been committed. If all that was required was a few hours of Sarahle's time, they were willing to cooperate.

"Now, what do you have in mind for me to do?" Sarahle asked briskly, coming right to the point.

"Keep an eye on the lab," Alex answered, equally concisely. "I'll get you a lab coat. It will help you fit in."

"But there are lots of people around who aren't wearing one. You're not wearing one," she said dubiously, eying his open-necked dark blue shirt.

"Sometimes I wear one," he told her, "if I'm doing something particularly dirty, or if the lab is cold. If you're wearing a lab coat, no one will wonder what you're doing here."

"Okay," she said, putting on the white coat. "Now what? What am I doing here?"

He looked at her speculatively for a moment and decided. "You're a lab technician I just hired. Whenever anyone is looking, just watch what I'm doing, as if you were going to have to do it yourself tomorrow.

"I'll have to leave at eleven to teach a class, and in any case I have to give Elisha a chance to set his trap. Watch for him while I'm gone, and if anyone comes in, be sure to notice everything he touches. And don't touch any of those things yourself!"

"Where shall I be?" she asked. "So I can watch the lab without being noticed?"

"You can sit at the desk in that cubbyhole," he told her, indicating the tiny annex at the end of the room, away from the door. "If you see anyone come in, you can get up and stand behind the file cabinet. He won't be able to see you there unless he goes all the way in, but you can peek out as soon as you think it's safe."

"Okay," she said cheerfully. "I'm all set. How do I recognize Elisha, if he comes in?"

"All that comes to mind is that he's big, fat, and ugly," Alex said. "Will that do?"

"That's fine," she said. "That means there's no chance of mistaking him for you."

"No," he said, with a quizzical glance.

Micky came in while Alex was still in the lab. "I passed the word about the power supply," he reported, "and I must say, I was brilliant! It's not such a simple thing to do in a natural way, when you stop to think about it, but I believe I came up with a good approach. I maneuvered to be within earshot of Elisha, and said to Yekeziel, 'I'm afraid we might soon lose another member of the department. Alex has a high-voltage power supply that short circuits, and he insists on using it anyway.' I told him that I offered to help you find a replacement for this evening, but that you didn't want to bother. I'm sure Elisha was paying attention."

"Good. Thanks," Alex said.

"If anything happens to you," Micky warned him, "I lose both my friend and my wife. She's not talking to me until this is over, because she thinks that if I had supported her we could have talked you out of it." He touched Alex on the shoulder on his way out. "Be careful now, little brother."

"Adi was pretty severe with me, too," Sarahle confided when Micky had gone. "I had to promise to do a good job of protecting you."

"Protecting me?" Alex asked, amused at the size of his protector.

"I have a gun in my handbag," Sarahle said quietly.

"You won't leave it lying around?" Alex reminded her.

"I know the rules, reservist," she chided, meaning that while Alex was presumably an army reservist serving one month a year, she was a professional security officer. The chiding was gentle, because Sarahle's outstanding asset as a police officer was her ability to judge character, and she had instantly placed Alex as someone who would have a responsible job in the army.

Her mental classification was automatic and didn't require conscious thought, but in this case Adi's description of the situation had added to the respect she felt. Alex would have been surprised to know that the two women were firmly convinced that he was putting his life in danger for no other reason than to protect Miriam, a woman he had never even met.

He showed Sarahle the power supply, a gray metal box about the size of a stereo receiver sitting on a shelf above one of the workbenches. "This can produce two thousand volts," he told her. "These red and black wires coming out of it are connected to the electrophoresis tank to start a run. You connect them first, then turn the power on and adjust the voltage and current. But you see that the on and off positions aren't marked on the switch. If they were ever marked, the markings wore off before I got the machine. So I go by the red light that goes on with the power.

"If I wanted to kill someone with this I would unscrew the light, loosen the base of the voltage indicator needle, and leave the power on at maximum voltage and current. It wouldn't take more than a minute."

Sarahle nodded slowly, looking soberly at the deceptive little apparatus, and, seeing that she understood, Alex went back to his work. At eleven he gave her a quick smile on his way out, and she saluted jauntily, returning the smile, and went to her hiding place.

Several students accompanied him back to the lab after class and he answered their questions patiently. As soon as the last one had left, he went to Sarahle. "Any news?" he asked.

She shook her head. "You are nervous after all!" she said.

"Is that the word for it?" he asked with mock seriousness. "I feel like a bullfighter who has just entered the ring for the first time and doesn't know from which direction to expect the bull. I suppose you're used to this kind of thing."

"Not really," she said. "There was a time when I used to traipse around in high heels and a miniskirt, trapping pimps and drug pushers, but that's not quite the same."

"The outfit is different, at least," Alex agreed. He was busy preparing the samples for the evening's run and didn't look at her as he spoke, so Sarahle was left wondering whether the joke was intentional.

The samples consisted of material he had removed from a minus-seventy-degree freezer in the corridor and divided among a series of tiny plastic tubes, using a pipette with disposable tips that he changed for each sample. To each tube he added a few drops of various solutions that he took from the refrigerator in the lab.

He looked at his watch as he put several of the sample tubes in a bright yellow plastic rack and set it afloat in a heated water bath. The remaining tubes waited in a black rubber bucket full of ice.

"I have half an hour now," he said. "I'll get us some lunch."

He brought sandwiches and Coca-Cola from the snack bar on the first floor, and they ate in the cubbyhole, Sarahle sitting in the desk chair and Alex on another wooden chair pulled in from the lab.

"Would you tell me about your work?" she asked. "I'd be interested to know what you're doing. But I warn you I don't know any biochemistry!"

"We have two projects in the lab," he told her. "One I do for love, and the other for money. What I want to work on is the trigger of DNA replication. It's important, it's fascinating, and it's exciting, because I'm making progress with the system I work on. The experiment I'm setting up now is part of that project.

"The trouble is, the equipment and supplies I need are very expensive. It's almost impossible to get money for basic research, so I have to come up with a proposal for something that will produce practical results faster.

"I work with bacilli, and one of the things I know how to do with them is genetic engineering. What I'm doing for the money is combining genes from two varieties of insect-killing bacillus to make a strain that should be better at protecting grain supplies.

"It's only interesting as a technical problem, but I don't mind doing it. I feel guilty being paid, however badly, for doing something I love. I only wish it didn't take up so much of my time."

"Then what you really like doing is detective work!" Sarahle exclaimed. "You have to know the truth."

Alex shook his head. "It sounds admirable," he said, "but I don't think it's true."

"Why not?" Sarahle persisted. "That's exactly what you're doing now."

"It's not the same thing," Alex said. "Some questions fascinate me, and I suppose I would do almost anything to get the answer. But not questions about who did what to whom. I know someone has to answer them, but I don't feel any compulsion to do it myself." After pausing to consider he added, "That doesn't mean it might not be important to me in a particular case."

The half hour was up, and the samples required some further treatment. He had just finished and put them in the refrigerator when a tall young man came in.

"Here's Arik," Alex said, getting to his feet. "I don't want him in the lab, and I have to get out of the way myself. I'll stay away for the next couple of hours."

Alex insisted on taking his surprised doctoral student to the coffee room for a discussion, even though they had nothing of particular importance to discuss. Afterward, with Arik safely off the premises, he went to the library to look over the newly arrived journals. Nothing in them was exciting enough to compete with the thought that Elisha might be arranging his death. Finally he realized that he had no idea what he had been reading during the past half hour. It was almost five.

From the doorway of the lab he saw Elisha standing in front of the bench, facing the power supply. Elisha turned at the sound of his footsteps. A momentary hesitation showed that he was disconcerted.

"Oh, Alex," he said, with a smile, "I heard you've been having some trouble with this, and I thought I might be able to help."

By the time he had finished the sentence Alex was beside him, standing with his hands in his pockets and studying Elisha's face with an unreadable expression on his own.

Gaining confidence, Elisha continued, "I've succeeded in fixing mine in the past, so I thought I would give you the benefit of my experience. Connect it up, will you, and let me see what's wrong. I just walked in and I haven't touched it yet."

"Haven't you?" Alex asked.

"That's a lie!" Sarahle shouted, appearing suddenly from the annex at the end of the room, dark eyes flashing, the unbuttoned lab coat flapping around her, and the large black handbag clutched incongruously to one side.

Elisha stepped back and gave Alex a powerful shove that should have made him fall forward onto the workbench. Rather than resisting, Alex twisted away. He saw that the black and red wires were lying in a puddle of liquid that hadn't been there when he left.

Elisha had too much momentum to check himself. He instinctively broke his fall with two large hands that landed in the sinister puddle. There was a crackling sound, and he twitched convulsively and collapsed on the floor like a felled ox.

Sarahle rushed to kneel at his side, and she turned a distressed face to Alex. "We should try to give him mouth-to-mouth resuscitation," she said. "But he's so big! Do you know how to do it?"

"I know how to do it," Alex said, remaining where he stood and not removing his hands from his pockets. "But there's no point in it. Look at his face." Elisha must have poured an efficiently conducting salt solution on the benchtop, and the current flowing through his chest when he put both hands in it had given him a massive heart attack. After a moment, having seen all he wanted to of the remains of Elisha, he unplugged the power supply.

Sarahle's presence helped, but it still took four hours before the police left, and Alex and Sarahle were sitting in Micky and Adi's living room. Sarahle was amazed that after the police were through, Alex had returned the power supply to its normal condition and turned it on to run his samples overnight.

They were all relieved that it was finally over and that no one except Elisha had been hurt, but they didn't want to celebrate his death. Still, it had been a long day and everyone was hungry, so Adi put out bread, cheese, olives, and sliced cucumbers and tomatoes, and made them filter coffee. The real coffee was meant for Alex, of course, an offering which he acknowledged by a smile and a kiss on the cheek when Adi served it to him.

The three of them were going over all the details, filling in missing information for each other, but Alex had little to contribute. He could gauge the level of nervous tension he had been under all day by how tired he felt now.

"Aren't you glad?" Adi asked him during a momentary lull.

"I wanted to stop Elisha," Alex replied slowly, "but I didn't want to do it this way. I feel like an executioner, and I don't like the feeling."

"But he was trying as hard as he could to murder you!" Sarahle cried. "In fact, he nearly succeeded!"

He nodded. "I know," he agreed. "But I had planned it that way. I put us both in that situation, even though I couldn't control all the details."

Micky brusquely closed the subject. "He was an evil, murdering monster, and he killed himself with the setup he had arranged for you. Don't start feeling guilty simply because you were smarter than he was."

"I would have liked unassailable proof that he killed Ilan," Alex said almost wistfully, earning a hard look from his friend.

"But it's clear now that he did!" Adi objected.

It was Micky who answered. "It looks that way," he conceded, "but strictly speaking, it remains unproven. Do you have any reason to doubt it?" he asked Alex.

"It's still conceivable that it was an ordinary accident," Alex replied, "or—"

"Or what?" Micky wanted to know.

"I don't know," Alex admitted, begging the question with a partial truth, "but I would have been much happier if Elisha had stayed alive and confessed."

"You'd better watch that curiosity of yours, young man!" Micky said with a stern, avuncular air. "Some day, if you're not careful, it could get you into real trouble!" Both Micky and Alex laughed uncontrollably.

After an hour or so, Alex summoned the energy to pull himself out of his chair and go home. He checked on Daniel, who was sleeping peacefully, then took a long shower and went to bed. Varda was already asleep, and he would leave in the morning before she got up, as usual. There was no reason to expect that the subject of Elisha would ever come up between them.

CHAPTER 14

Varda came home from a party after midnight on a Tuesday evening, expecting to find Alex either already asleep or reading something in one of his strange languages. But this time he had company. He had mentioned earlier that a childhood friend from Budapest had turned up, but it had slipped her mind until she saw the two of them, flushed and laughing, sitting on the floor with an almost empty bottle on the low table between them.

Varda's gleaming red hair swirled over her shoulders as she burst into the room, wearing a low-cut black jersey and black pants. She would have stopped traffic at any intersection in the world, and Alex's friend looked at her with flattering surprised pleasure.

"This is Yantsi," Alex said to Varda. "Yantsi, this is Varda, my wife."

"I kiss your hand, my lady," Yantsi said with feeling. He clearly would have liked to suit the action to the words, but awkwardly placed as he was, and with almost half a bottle of the Hungarian brandy he had brought working against it, it wasn't a practical idea.

Varda looked questioningly at Alex. "My wife doesn't understand a word of Hungarian," he informed Yantsi, who hadn't paid attention to the fact that Alex had introduced him in English.

Alex didn't know how much English Yantsi knew, and in any case would have liked to continue the conversation in Hungarian. He had liked Yantsi a lot as a boy; he was intelligent, good natured, and full of fun. He was in Jerusalem to attend a gathering of specialists in ethnic music. Alex was glad to celebrate the occasion with him. He hoped Varda wouldn't stay.

She did stay, though, because Yantsi was a very handsome man, big and ruddy faced, with sparkling dark eyes, a mane of black hair, and a long black mustache. It was presumably worth putting up with some language difficulties in order to bask in his admiration.

"I'm very happy to meet you," Yantsi repeated in correct but strongly accented English. The polite English expression wasn't nearly as romantic as the standard Hungarian greeting, but Yantsi put equal feeling into it. Varda smiled happily and settled down on the couch near Alex.

"What were you talking about?" she asked Yantsi.

"We talked about the situation in Hungary," he told her, "and the people we both used to know in Budapest. Do you remember Madam Popov?" he asked, turning to Alex. "Did you know that she died very soon after you went away? We decided it was you who sent her to an early grave."

"What are you talking about?" Alex exclaimed.

"Your famous entrance to her class," Yantsi said with a broad smile.

"Ah," Alex said in reply.

"Madam Popov taught Russian," Yantsi explained to Varda, "when we were about twelve years old. We didn't like her. She used to insult us and the Hungarian language. And nobody wanted to learn Russian anyway.

"One day she got mad at 'Aleksandrrr,' because he thought of some things you could say in Hungarian that you couldn't say in Russian. She wouldn't admit that he was right. She told him to leave the class and never to come through the door again! So he went out. She almost had a heart attack ten minutes later, when he came back in— through the window!"

Yantsi noticed that Varda hadn't understood the point. "Did I forget to say?" he asked. "The class was on the third floor! How did you do it?" he asked Alex. "You never told me."

"I climbed down from the roof," Alex told him. It had been a long time ago and he didn't remember much about it except the highlights. Those had been the enjoyable challenge of getting from the roof to the third-floor window, which had been tricky, and the amazement and horror on Madam Popov's face when he climbed in. It had made him wonder what impossible physical feat she thought had been required. It had also been the first time he had ever seen anyone actually change color. In retrospect, it was lucky that she hadn't had a heart attack.

He hadn't thought ahead and had no idea what she would do, but she just stood there, so after a moment he went to his place and sat down. She resumed the class as if nothing had happened and never referred to the incident, but the consensus was that she was marginally less insulting to Hungarians and their language afterward. Half the class thought this was because Alex had given her the unfortunate impression that they loved her class so much that nothing could keep them away; the other half felt that she was merely afraid that if she annoyed Alex, he would do it again.

"That was a silly thing to do," Varda commented.

"You're right," Alex said. "I won't do it anymore."

As he moved to lean back against the couch, his arm brushed Varda's knee and she squeezed his shoulder in response. Yantsi had begun another story, and she nodded and smiled at him, though it wasn't clear how much she understood. She may not have been listening closely, since she had begun to caress the back of her husband's neck under the collar of his shirt, leaning forward now and then so that her silken, perfumed hair touched his cheek.

His pulse quickened in a physiological reaction that was completely beyond his control. When she put her arms around him and gently pulled his head to her breast with a quick hug, the need to turn and embrace her was overpowering, and he refilled his glass in order to move away.

He mustn't touch Varda again, he thought, letting the conversation continue over his head as a meaningless babble, without bothering to understand even a word of it. That was even clearer to him now than when sober. He couldn't stand to experience another time the emotional whipsaw that was an inescapable part of making love to her.

The instinct for self-preservation made him try to avoid

physical contact with her, but the more he tried to avoid it, the harder she made it for him. It was an unequal contest that whether he won or lost, he always lost.

Once all resistance had ended and the victory was clearly hers, she would make him almost believe that she loved him with all her heart, although he knew that it wasn't true, and that even if it had been, it was too late. Why did she want to say things that they both knew were lies, he would ask himself? And then he would wonder if it was only he who realized that they were lies.

It was impossible not to respond to her when she was so loving and beautiful, although he knew that the woman he had originally fallen in love with had never really existed. Her very self-centredness gave her an almost childlike innocence, so that when he held her in his arms he wanted to shield her from the painful knowledge that people die, that a body broken and repaired is never the same again, that a betrayed trust can be forgiven, but not forgotten.

No matter how intimately embraced, they were a thousand miles apart, and he would wish that he could talk to her, that he knew what she thought, that he could feel that he was more to her than a male body, easily replaceable by another.

In those moments when all thought was driven from his head by the intensity of physical sensation, he knew that there was nothing he wouldn't do, give, or promise, just to be able to stay where he was. But when they were past, he would feel—violated. Because he had surrendered himself so abjectly to this woman he lived with, who in every important way was a stranger, and who cared for him no more than for a pet dog. Because of the wrenching dichotomy between what he thought and felt at all other times and the feelings called forth, against his will, when she clung to him and caressed him and covered his face and body with kisses.

Finally, long after Varda had fallen asleep, he would be left in a turmoil of confused and conflicting emotions, certain of nothing except that he couldn't live like this.

The solution was simple; all he had to do was to remove himself from this impossible situation. Only that would mean leaving Daniel behind to cope with Varda on his own, because there was no way for them to leave together.

He had tried, although he knew that it wouldn't work. It was a few days after he had come home from the hospital, and he was sitting at the kitchen table while Varda bustled around him making soup.

"I hope you appreciate the trouble I'm going to for you," she had said. "Between you and Daniel, I haven't had a free minute to work all week."

"We could move out," he had offered. "Right away, if you like. I know you don't want to be bothered taking care of us, and it isn't necessary." He didn't know where he would find the money for such an arrangement, but he would manage it if only she would agree.

"We would come to visit you whenever you liked, instead of being underfoot all the time," he had added, trying to make the offer as enticing as possible.

"Alex!" she had exclaimed reproachfully. "Don't be silly! Of course I don't want you to move out! And my son will leave over my dead body."

★   ★   ★

His thoughts had now completed the full, useless, disheartening circuit, and he didn't want to go on with them. He decided that if he found himself crying into his brandy, it was time to stop drinking.

Eventually, tired of the strain of speaking English with Yantsi and losing hope of involving Alex in amorous games, Varda went to bed. Yantsi, inspecting the brandy bottle and finding a little left, offered it to Alex.

"I've had my share," Alex told him. "Whatever's left is yours."

Yantsi shook his head sorrowfully. "You're a great disappointment to me," he said. "I used to admire you very much at school. You were so smart and serious, but then, just when I would begin to worry that you were hopeless, suddenly you would do something really interesting!" They both laughed, reminded again of Madam Popov. "And now look what's become of you," Yantsi continued scornfully. "A university professor!"

"I'm not a professor," Alex corrected him.

"Not yet, you mean. And definitely not a serious drinker."

"Nobody's perfect," Alex said philosophically.

At two thirty Varda came back in her pajamas to find Alex by himself, still sitting on the floor, but now surrounded with papers and using the coffee table as a support for the notebook in which he was writing.

"What are you doing?" she asked. "It's the middle of the night! Where's Yantsi?"

"I put him in a taxi," he told her. "I still have some work to do for my lecture tomorrow morning."

"You're in no condition to prepare a lecture!" she exclaimed.

"Why not?" he asked.

"I thought you were drunk," she said.

That was an exaggeration, he thought, but not worth arguing about.

"If I was," he replied, "I'm not anymore."

Since he was obviously waiting for her to leave so he could go back to his papers, she went back to bed.

Chapter 15

Two weeks after Elisha's death Orli, his graduate student, requested an appointment with David Shiloh. He had been asked to take over the direction of Elisha's students.

David had no idea why Elisha had been fooling around with a high-voltage power supply in Alex's lab, and he was not much interested in finding out. Elisha had been loud and self-assured, while Ilan had been quiet and pedantic. However, David had privately faulted both for scoffing at basic safety measures, ignoring not only the random warnings on the little signs but also precautions any reasonable person would take. They had shared the common Israeli belief that accidents happened to other people. They were much too smart ever to have an accident themselves. It didn't particularly surprise David that either one had come to grief, although it was remarkable that the deaths had occurred within less than two months of each other.

That afternoon, when Orli entered his office, David found the formalities a bit awkward. He was well aware that she had been Elisha's mistress, but officially she had been related to him only as student to professor and there was no reason for her to be incapacitated with grief. He was relieved to find that she wanted to get right to work, opening her lab notebook and beginning to describe her latest series of experiments.

She told him she had been having trouble with her immunoassays. There seemed to be a technical problem. The protein she wanted to look at could no longer be found where it had always appeared.

"I'm using the same antibody preparation I used before," she said, "and I know the protein is there. Why can't I see it anymore?"

Orli's question suggested too great a dependence on her adviser for a student at her stage of doctoral studies, David thought, suppressing a sigh. As she said, this appeared to be a purely technical problem and the solution could only be arrived at by carefully going over the details of her experimental procedures. It would be much easier for her to do this than for anyone else, no matter how knowledgeable or experienced. He foresaw a long and boring session trying to help her do what she should be perfectly capable of doing by herself.

Oh well, thought Professor Shiloh, who would have been embarrassed to learn that the students and younger members of the department considered him to be a silver-haired Sir Galahad, ever a pushover for a maiden in distress. Poor little thing, perhaps this isn't the time for her to learn to be more independent. Controlling his impatience, he set himself to the job of scrutinizing the notebook in front of him.

"I see this experiment was done on the sixteenth of April," he said. "I gather that was the last time you did the immunoassay, and it wasn't successful."

"I can't understand it. I did everything just as usual, but it doesn't work anymore."

"When was the first time it didn't succeed?" David asked patiently.

Orli picked up her notebook and began to flip the pages. "Here it is," she said, handing the book back to him. "March fourth."

"The fourth of March. According to your notes, you added the goat antirabbit antibody at nine P.M. Then you must have been here when Ilan had the accident," David said, lifting his eyes from the page with a questioning look. It wasn't important, of course, but he had had the impression that everyone who had been in the building at the time of the explosion had arrived shortly afterward to investigate. Either that, or within the next few days they had sought out the three who had been first on the scene to tell them what they had heard, what they had thought, and what had kept them from coming.

"I wasn't here," Orli told him. "It was Elisha. He offered to finish the experiment for me so I could go home. I had started very early in the morning," she added defensively.

"I see," said David, although he didn't.

"And Elisha followed your protocol exactly?" he asked. "All the incubation times were the same? All the reagents?"

The expression on her face told him he had struck paydirt.

"Oh!" she exclaimed. "I feel so stupid! I apologize for wasting your time. I should have thought of it, but I still haven't . . ." she trailed off, and for an awful moment he thought the façade of self-control was about to crumble and that she would burst into tears.

Instead, she recovered and began to explain. "I had used up the last of a batch of goat antibody in the experiment before this one," she said. This generic antibody was crucial to the immunoassay. Its role was to bind to the specific antibody that Orli had produced by innoculating a rabbit with her protein. At the end of the assay there would be a series of molecules bound to each other: protein; antibody to the protein; antibody to the first antibody. The commercially available goat antibody to rabbit proteins, the last molecule in the series, came with an attached chemical group that caused it to turn blue when treated with certain reagents, thereby making the protein of interest visible wherever it was present.

"I thought we had another bottle," she continued. "Actually, Elisha had told me only the day before that we did, but he must have been mistaken, because we couldn't find it on the day of the experiment.

"It was almost six o'clock by the time we realized there was a problem, but Elisha told me to just go and not to worry, he would take care of it. He happened to know that Ilan had a bottle of goat antirabbit antibody in his refrigerator, and he would just go in and take it!" Orli said this in a tone that was full of admiration for the brilliant and innovative idea of walking into someone else's lab and helping oneself to anything useful that might be found there.

David wondered whether Elisha had made a habit of stealing from other labs. Even if he had, he was merely a scientific adviser to his students, not a guru of life and morals, and they were old enough to know better. He was beginning to feel less sympathetic toward Orli.

"I see," he said again. "So this was a different batch of goat antibody than in your previous experiments. If Elisha just took it from Ilan's refrigerator without speaking to anybody, he wouldn't know if it was spoiled. And you've been using this bottle ever since. Neither you nor Elisha bothered to return it to Ilan's lab, so if they knew that it was no good, they never had a chance to tell you about it."

"Yes," Orli agreed. "That must have been what happened. I had forgotten that it wasn't our bottle, because I didn't take it myself. Elisha always knew how to take care of everything." Her lips started to tremble again, and she abruptly stood up and left the room.

The entire session with Orli had been disturbing, but David put it out of his mind and went back to his own work. It was only when he woke the following morning that he realized what had bothered him.

As soon as he arrived at the department he knocked on Nahum Bron's open office door to announce himself and walked in. He had known Nahum long enough to dispense with formalities, so he got right to the point. "Nahum," he said, as the other looked up over his reading glasses, "do you remember when I was standing with you and Alex at Ilan's funeral, and Elisha joined us?"

"Why shouldn't I remember?" Nahum began testily. "I'm not entirely senile yet. Look at this head of black hair! I'm practically a baby compared to you, with that silver mop. Very distinguished looking, of course, but much more likely to cover a deteriorating brain."

"Calm yourself, Nahum," David responded with a defensive gesture. "I just asked a simple question. Though come to think of it," he continued judiciously, looking down at the top of Nahum's head from his vantage point as he stood in front of the desk, "isn't that head of black hair getting a little thin at the crown?" Nahum was able to bring out the worst even in David Shiloh.

After enough insults had been traded to satisfy the inexplicable needs of Nahum's prickly personality, he had no trouble remembering the occasion in question. He was certain that Elisha had explicitly denied being in the building at the time of the explosion in which Ilan had lost his life.

"That's the way I remember it, too," David said in a puzzled tone. "But now listen to this." And he proceeded to describe his interview with Orli. "So you see," he concluded, "there's no doubt that Elisha was here. I wonder why he denied it?"

"Now, there's a question for you," Nahum said in a tone that was completely serious. "I could answer it, but I prefer to leave the reporting to the man who did the experiment. Drop in Saturday afternoon. I know some people who will be fascinated by what you have to say."

Alex was curious about why Nahum had invited him to come by on Saturday afternoon. Nahum would only say that he had some new information that Alex would be glad to hear. With that warning, Alex left Daniel at home.

Nahum lived not more than ten minutes' drive from Alex, in the neighborhood called the German Colony, from the time in the late nineteenth century when German Lutherans settled there. The land where they had built their houses was known as Emek Refaim, the Valley of the Giants, for a tribe of giants mentioned in the Old Testament.

Although many of the original old houses in the German Colony had given way to apartment buildings, some lovely spots were still to be found there. Nahum and Sonia lived in one such place, a small apartment tucked behind one of the older buildings. Alex pushed open a green wooden gate and followed a stone path around the apartment building and through a small garden of flowering geraniums and roses. Mint and verbena, for fragrant teas, bracketed Nahum's front door.

Micky and Adi were already there, and the others arrived soon afterward. The guests were greeted by Sonia, a birdlike woman with sparkling dark eyes rather like her husband's and a sleek bun of steel-gray hair.

It was the first time Alex and Miriam had met. She was a pleasant-looking middle-aged woman, neither short nor tall, neither thin nor fat. Sonia introduced Alex to her and they shook hands, neither being sure that it was the most appropriate form of greeting for the occasion.

David Shiloh entered the living room, not knowing quite what to expect, and found Alex, Micky, Adi, Miriam Tal, and Sarahle already there. Micky introduced him to Sarahle, and Nahum and Sonia served coffee before Nahum brought up the subject that had brought them together.

Alex and Micky had suspected Elisha of arranging Ilan's

"accident," he told David, and it seemed they were right. "That explains why Elisha didn't want it known that he was in the building at the time. He wanted to avoid suspicion. Since apparently no one saw him, there was no reason, under normal circumstances, why it should ever have come out.

"But now, because of Elisha's death, we've found proof that not only was he in the building on the night Ilan died, he was even in Ilan's lab. Tell them about your talk with Orli, David."

When David had finished, Alex told him the rest of the story, ending with the explanation of how he and Micky, with the help of Miriam, Adi, Sarahle, and Sonia Bron, had set a trap with Alex as the bait.

"I apologize for not telling you exactly what we were doing at the time," Alex told Miriam. "I didn't want you to feel responsible if something went wrong." Something had gone wrong, and it was he who was responsible. "And," he added, "I thought it would make it easier for you to be convincing when you spoke to Elisha."

"Please don't apologize!" Miriam exclaimed. "After that business with the gun, I was scared to death of Elisha. I gave him everything he wanted in the divorce. I was too shocked to fight about anything; it came as a complete surprise to me when he left. So he certainly had no reason to harm me. But I knew that he had tried to kill me that evening, and I was sure he would try again. Only the police wouldn't believe me. You saved my life."

"Unfortunately," Alex finished, "he died in his own trap, so we were left without conclusive proof of his guilt.

With what you've told us, the case against him has become much stronger."

"The evidence would convict him in any court," Nahum asserted. He enumerated the points in the case against Elisha.

"First of all, the 'accident' in Ilan's lab happened the day after Miriam told Elisha that Ilan was about to send a letter that would ruin him. And we know for sure that he was in the building that evening, and that he was in Ilan's lab, and that he lied about it.

"Then he tried to kill Miriam a few weeks later. There was no reason for him to suddenly decide that he needed to get rid of her, unless he was afraid that she would go to someone else with the information that was in that letter Ilan was writing. And last, when he thought that Alex was about to send the very same letter, he immediately tried to get rid of him, too. It couldn't be any clearer.

"And there's one more little detail I can add," Nahum said. "After hearing what David had to say, I went directly to Ilan's lab and asked Rafi" (he was Ilan's doctoral student, Nahum explained for the benefit of those who didn't work in the department) "whether they happened to have some denatured goat antirabbit antibody. Naturally, he thought it was a very peculiar request. 'Why do you ask?' he said. 'Does someone want some denatured antibody?' But then he said that as a matter of fact they had a bottle that Ilan had mailed to himself express from Copenhagen, that had taken three weeks to arrive. It was last summer, and by the time it reached them it was completely useless. He opened the refrigerator to get it for me, but it wasn't there. 'Someone must finally have thrown it out,' he said."

The following Saturday Micky and Adi wanted Alex and Daniel to go with them to Ein Feshcha, on the Dead Sea, so the children could swim in the sweet spring water. It was pleasantly warm there now, but in another few weeks it would be too hot to stand. Alex thought it was a good idea, provided they could return well before evening. It had been too long since his last visit to Yehudit and Akiva, and he was anxious to talk to them.

Late afternoon found Alex and Daniel, a little sunburned in spite of all their precautions, in Yehudit's plant-filled living room, eating linzer torte.

Mina and Elchanan, the psychologists who lived down the street, were there. Alex waited until they left and Daniel went to play outside.

"Do you mind if I tell you a rather long story?" he asked Akiva.

"Please do," Akiva replied. This was quite unusual, coming from Alex.

"Do you remember our discussion of ill-wishing?" Alex asked. "I told you at the time that someone in the department had died, and that an astonishing number of people had good reason to be glad about it. Of all the people who might have wished this fellow dead, including myself, there was one who had a motive strong enough to kill for.

"That man is also dead now, and we can't hear his side of it, but it seems certain that he actually did murder the first man." The same instinct that would have prevented Alex from telling his mother about his role in the accumulation of the evidence warned him not to mention it to Yehudit and Akiva. An explanation of how Elisha had died would probably upset them, and would certainly distract them from the point.

"But there was someone else," he went on, "who had good reason to hate Ilan and who willed him to die exactly as he did. And who learned about his death from a dream she had the same night that it happened, while she was at the other end of the country. Hard as it was to accept that her wish could have led to his death, it's almost as hard to believe that what she described was pure coincidence."

Akiva wanted to know more, and Alex told him about Shosh's wish and the dream she had dreamt in Eilat. "What do you think?" he said. "Could they really mean nothing at all?"

"Now I'll tell you a story," Akiva countered. "Many years ago two thieves managed to break into an underground chamber of an ancient castle near Prague. They stole some extremely valuable objects that had belonged to the family for hundreds of years. The owner of the castle still lived in it at that time. It was well before the communists took over and sent him to work in the uranium mines.

"The incident was reported in the newspapers, together with the count's prediction that the thieves wouldn't have the objects for long—they had been presented to his ancestors in reward for heroism in battle, and although they had been stolen more than once in the past, they had invariably been returned.

"Not long afterward, I read that one of the thieves had turned himself in to the police and confessed to the crime. He told them that his companion had died suddenly of a mysterious illness, and that he himself had suffered a series of near fatal accidents that had made him fear for his life if he didn't return the stolen objects. He was illiterate, by the way, and didn't know anything about the count's prediction.

"Naturally, popular superstition immediately decided there was a family curse attached to those objects. At first I laughed at the gullibility of all those uneducated people. But then I asked myself what it meant to say there was a family curse. Wasn't it really just saying that the head of the family at that time, and maybe also some of his ancestors, had the ability to mount a psychic attack on the thieves? How could I rule it out? Anyone who has lived long enough has come across examples of incidents like that. It has to make you think."

"The story the girl told me definitely made me think," Alex replied. "But the man only died once. They couldn't both have killed him. And it looks as if the real killer was anything but ectoplasmic."

From his point of view, the time had come to close the file on the subject of wish-killing. It was frustrating that in spite of his best efforts he had been unable even to arrive at a completely satisfying negative proof, and had to be content with circumstantial evidence that in this case it wasn't a psychic attack but Elisha who had been responsible for the murder. Having tried every reasonable means, or, according to Nahum, even an unreasonable one, to settle the question, there was nothing more he could do.

"Of course," Akiva said, "if you've found your murderer, then that settles it. The man was killed by normal, everyday means. I would have been interested to meet this man who had people waiting in line to kill him."

They were silent for a moment until Yehudit, who had listened attentively to the entire conversation without contributing one word, stood up and smoothed her skirt. "The best thing is not to give people good reasons to murder you," she said. "After all, whether they can do it by thought or have to get their hands dirty, it's all the same for the victim. Either way, he's dead. Now, how about another piece of linzer torte?"

Chapter 16

Alex was invited to give a talk on bacterial phosphorylation at a meeting in Lausanne in October. Initially he decided not to go. The organizers would pay his expenses, but he didn't want to take the time off. Also, it was scheduled for shortly after the beginning of the school year, a bad time to find a replacement for the course he was giving.

He finally did go, because it was an opportunity to make final decisions about the research proposal he had been discussing for the past few months with Hildegard Kraus, the German professor he had met in Athens the previous spring. She had convinced him to go to Lausanne when she told him that she would also be there and would keep herself free for their project. The deadline for submitting the grant request was approaching, and they were at a stage when a face-to-face meeting would save a lot of time and effort.

He had remembered Hildegard as a self-assured blond beauty, so it took him a moment to recognize her when he saw her in Lausanne. She was still blond and still beautiful, but so pale and subdued that she seemed a different person. For an instant he was afraid that she was ill, but in fact it was Richard, her husband. A few days before the meeting he had suddenly felt unwell, and had quickly been scheduled for coronary bypass surgery. The operation was to be done the following week.

Lausanne wasn't so far from Frankfurt. That was the only reason she hadn't canceled their arrangement, she said. She called home every morning and evening, and she warned Alex that if Richard gave her the least cause for worry she would hop on the next plane, no matter at what stage they happened to be in at hammering out their proposal.

In fact he had sounded weak to her one morning and she was gone within the hour, missing her own lecture that was scheduled for the following day. Although they had nearly finished their discussions by that time, there was still a lot of work to be done by each of them at home, writing down their ideas in polished form and describing all the experiments they intended to do in great detail.

To Alex, writing the experimental section of a research proposal was a particularly annoying chore. Funding agencies required detailed descriptions of methodology in order to weed out proposals that hadn't been well thought out. Unfortunately it was neither easy nor very useful for the person who intended to do the work to foresee all the necessary details of the techniques he envisioned using months, or even years, before he would need them. It was even less useful if, as could well happen, the research led in an unexpected direction and an entirely different set of experiments was eventually required.

They had intended to divide this section between them. Under the circumstances, Hildegard would be pressed for time during the coming weeks, so Alex offered to do it all.

She made only a token show of being unwilling to take advantage of him.

It made Alex brood about life's unfairness. His own wife didn't give a damn about him, so why should he always be the one to suffer from other women's devotion to their husbands?

By February, when they heard that the proposal had been accepted, he had forgotten all about his minor sacrifice. Hildegard remembered, though. When she called to exchange congratulations with him she sounded so grateful, and even affectionate, that he would cheerfully have written any number of research proposals for her.

The following May Sarahle and her boyfriend got married. Sarahle was a Yemenite, and her boyfriend, a fellow policeman, was a Moroccan. That meant that there was a henna party a few days before the wedding. The Jews from Arab countries had adopted the custom of daubing red dye on the palms of the bride and groom to bring them good luck. In Israel it would often be done at a party where the bride and groom, and sometimes other members of their families as well, would be dressed in the traditional costume of their land of origin.

As one of Sarahle's friends, Alex was naturally invited to the henna party as well as to the wedding. He and Sarahle didn't see each other often, but their shared experience gave them the feeling of having been in battle together. In Sarahle, the feeling was so strong that she often greeted him by jumping to her feet and saying, "Sir!" with a snappy salute. Fortunately she didn't do it at her henna party.

The party was in the garden of Sarahle's grandmother, who had a house in Ein Kerem, originally an Arab village but now a western suburb of Jerusalem. There was lots of delicious ethnic food; spicy salads, little pastries filled with meat, and sweets made with nuts and honey. They played tapes of Middle Eastern music and one of the groom's aunts, a woman of large proportions in a black dress, got up to dance. There was enthusiastic applause as soon as she appeared. A few other women and one of the men joined her in what was a slightly more modest, folk version of belly dancing.

There were at least fifty guests, but enough tables and chairs had been borrowed for all of them. Alex sat with Micky and Adi, admiring Sarahle. She was wearing a red gown embroidered with gold. Alex had never seen her wear makeup before, but now her lips were cherry red and her dark eyes seemed enormous. On her head was a tall golden crown, the traditional Yemenite bridal ornament.

Alex wouldn't have wanted to miss this, although Varda had tried very hard to take him with her that evening. A new gallery was opening in Tel Aviv, and there was to be a big party afterward at the elegant home of the gallery owner. "Everyone" would be there. Varda's "everyone" was Alex's "no one." There was no one at these parties for him to talk to. Among so many people some must certainly be interesting, but with the loud music, dim lights, and din of meaningless chatter, there was no way to tell.

There didn't seem to be much point to these parties, except as a mating game. They were certainly highly successful in that way. There was plentiful alcohol, although

Varda never drank any, and lots of slow dance music, so people could find out if they felt physically attracted to each other. Why did she like him to come with her—so that he could see how many of the men were attracted to her? He knew that she had never been "his," and he thought that he was reconciled to the idea. Still, he didn't like to see her flirting with them, and it must be obvious. Maybe she liked to watch him squirm when her female friends descended on him, like flies on fresh meat. Since he rarely went with Varda, he must represent an irresistible new challenge for them when he appeared. Unfortunately he wasn't interested in sexual conquests among Varda's friends.

After his last experience, it would be a long time before Varda would be able to persuade him to go again. After that party, while they were undressing for bed, she had asked him, "What did you think of Iris?"

"Who?" he had to ask.

"The blond girl. The wife of my friend Jo. I introduced you to her."

He remembered a small girl with pale blond hair. They had said hello to each other.

"What about her?" he asked.

"Would you like to go to bed with her?" was the next question.

"Jo and Iris and I were talking about it," she explained, seeing that he was too surprised to answer. "We thought it might be fun to all go to bed together, but Iris said she would have to see you before she agreed. Now she says it's all right. What do you say?"

"If you had mentioned it to me earlier, I would have

taken a better look at her," he said. "I didn't know you were interested in group sex."

She looked embarrassed. Naturally. He might have used the same tone to say, "I didn't know you liked to eat socks."

"I'm not, really," she said.

"If you are," he replied, "go right ahead. I'll pass."

He would have passed even if they hadn't put him in such a peculiar position. He had nothing against group sex in principle, he just hadn't given it any thought. It sounded as if it might be problematic anatomically, but probably something could be worked out.

The following spring he was invited to present a report of his work at a scientific meeting in New York. He booked a return flight with a stopover in Paris in order to visit his mother and sister.

He told them not to bother to meet him at the airport. It was easy to reach his mother's apartment by train carrying his one small suitcase. He transferred to the number four Metro line at the Gare du Nord and at the Gare de l'Est went out into the crisp, clear afternoon and walked to the familiar address on the Quai de Valmy facing the Canal St. Martin.

As the door opened, he was greeted simultaneously by the delicious odors of the festive dinner his mother was preparing and by the lady herself. She hugged and kissed him and exclaimed how happy she was to see him, how much she had missed him, and how thin he was. It was all entirely predictable and very satisfying.

He followed her into the kitchen where she served him strong coffee, which he scarcely had a chance to drink between answers to her questions. His mother was a handsome woman in her early sixties, with gray-blond hair and sparkling blue eyes. "You look wonderful!" he told her, observing her with pleasure across the kitchen table.

The conversation was in French. Although Simone, his mother, had learned Hungarian when she first went to Budapest to teach French, even before she met and married Egon Kertész, she had always spoken French to her two children. Privately, she considered Hungarian a barbaric language, and she didn't want to find herself unable to communicate properly with her own children because of an imperfect command of it. They had adapted easily to speaking French with her, but by preference spoke Hungarian with each other.

Alex showered quickly and hurriedly finished dressing. His sister Eva and her family had arrived. Kisses were exchanged all around and there was already a babble of voices as Eva and Guy, her husband, tried to carry on a conversation with Alex at the same time as the boys interjected remarks and Simone ran in and out of the kitchen, trying to finish her cooking without missing anything.

This was to be a family meal and no one else was expected except, of course, Grisha, their mother's long-time friend and neighbor, Grigori Sergeievitch. His septuagenarian aunt, Maria Borisovna, was staying with him this week, so she was also included.

"Look what Maria Borisovna has made in your honor, Sashinka," the tall old Russian proudly told Alex as he came in, holding out a china platter. On it rested a large cake covered in pale, creamy icing on which a regiment of toasted almond slices stood upright.

"This is a senatorski torte!" Grisha proclaimed, "the most delicious cake in the world! Only a few great Russian chefs still know how to make it."

Maria Borisovna, who was very short and very round, had lived in Paris for over forty years without learning more than a few words of French. She was beaming, and Alex quailed at what would now be his fate. *Bozse moi!* My God! he thought, trying to put himself in a Russian mode. Does this mean that I have to carry on a conversation with her in Russian?

Alex had studied the compulsory Russian in school in Budapest. But the Russians were hated and the compulsion was resented, so no one tried to actually learn the language. He decided to put off anything more demanding for the moment, and told the old lady as warmly as he could, *"Spasiba bolshoia,* thank you very much, Maria Borisovna!"

His mother served the sort of dinner a Parisienne produces on the occasion of a visit by her only son. The wines to accompany it had been brought by Guy, who was very knowledgeable about wines. His career as a corporate lawyer with an international clientele provided enough money to indulge this hobby, and in addition clients often sent him cases of special selections.

After a few glasses of excellent vintage, Alex felt sufficiently inspired to address two or three sentences to Maria Borisovna in Russian, to her great pleasure, and he acquitted himself creditably.

"But you speak very well, Sasha!" Grisha told him, smiling broadly. "I don't know why you pretend that you can't speak Russian!"

As soon as the cheese course that ended the meal was finished, the two teenage boys sprang out of their chairs. Michel, the younger, pulled Alex by the sleeve. "Come on, Alex," he pleaded. "You owe me a game of *Je te tiens*. You won last time, remember? It was during that famous ski trip last year, when you and Eric decided to get into the *Guiness Book of Records*. But I bet I can beat you now!"

He was referring to a game in which two people of any sex, with or without beards, face each other holding each other by the beard, if there is one, or by the chin if there isn't, and sing the following doggerel:

> *Je te tiens, tu me tiens, par la barbechette.*
> *Le premier de nous deux qui rira aura une tapette!*
> (I hold you, you hold me, by the little beard.
> The first one of us who laughs gets a slap!)

It is amazingly difficult to sit in that position, gazing solemnly into someone's eyes from a distance of inches, without laughing.

Alex went to sit on the carpet opposite Michel to start the game, but warned that he had an advantage this time. "Have you ever tried to make a zombie laugh, Michel?" he asked. "That's approximately the condition I'm in right now, so I would advise you to wait for a better opportunity if you want to win."

Guy came over to hand Alex a wineglass. "I want you to taste this, Alex," he said. "It's a really fine Sauterne."

"What are you trying to do to me?" Alex protested good-humoredly. "It was a wonderful meal with extraordinary wines, but I've had enough."

"Have mercy on him, Guy," his wife told him with an affectionate look, "You lawyers are a tough breed, but Alex is a delicate young man, and he's lost a night's sleep."

"You youngsters! You Frenchmen!" Grisha exploded contemptuously, though inaccurately. "None of you know how to drink! When I was in the Russian army, two of us would polish off a bottle of vodka between us every night!"

"You were in the Russian army, uncle Grisha?" Michel asked.

"Certainly!" their grandmother answered. "Didn't you know he received the medal of the Battle of Stalingrad?"

"Were you really in the Battle of Stalingrad, Uncle Grisha?" Eric asked.

"Of course not!" Grisha replied. "If I had actually been at Stalingrad I wouldn't be here to tell about it. My regiment was there and everyone in it was awarded the medal, but luckily for me I was elsewhere at the time."

The doorbell chimed, and another guest arrived. "Oh, Sylvie!" Alex's mother exclaimed. "I'm so glad you came in time to have dessert with us." Alex jumped to his feet and Sylvie ran to kiss him on both cheeks.

"I forgot to mention that Sylvie was coming," Alex's mother apologized. "We spoke on the telephone a few days ago and I told her you were arriving. She couldn't come for dinner, but I knew you would want her at least to drop in."

Shortly after Sylvie's arrival Eva and her mother served coffee and the fabulous cake. Grisha made a point of translating all the compliments for Maria Borisovna.

"Tell me about that ski trip last year," he said to Eric during a lull in the conversation. "I never heard anything about breaking records."

Eric looked apprehensively at his mother, and then to Alex for assistance, but Alex didn't say a word.

"Well," he began, "it was when Alex and I decided one day to try the black *piste,* the hardest way down. Only the weather began to close in while we were still at the top of the mountain. It was amazing! One minute—clear skies, and the next—we couldn't see even a few meters.

"It was funny, because we had started out pretty slowly. I guess Alex was thinking that he had his sister's firstborn son with him, and he didn't want to bring me home with broken arms and legs. And I was thinking that I had my mother's dear little brother with me, who was an old man of thirty-four and hadn't been skiing in years, and I didn't want to bring him home on a stretcher!

"Anyway, we saw what was happening and we just looked at each other, without saying a word, and took off like rockets! I've won a few races, in my age class, of course," he added modestly, "but I've never skied that fast in my life! The clouds were catching up with us anyway," he continued, "and we kept going off *piste* when the visibility would drop suddenly. We would barely miss going into the mountain, or off the mountain, only we were going at such speed, we couldn't have slowed down even if we wanted to, because the moment the sun was covered, the snow got all iced over.

"Once Alex missed the trail and went off into midair, in this mist where you couldn't see anything, and I didn't know when and if he was going to have something to land on!" He looked at Alex.

"It's a fact," Alex said, "that I've never been up in the air that long before without a parachute."

"*Mon Dieu!* Weren't you frightened?" Guy asked.

"Not at that particular moment," Alex answered. "I was too busy trying to remember which way was up."

Eric had forgotten about his mother for the moment, but she was looking grim, and his grandmother was absolutely horrified. They hadn't been told all these details before.

"But why didn't you just stop where you were at the top, instead of risking your lives like that?" his grandmother asked.

"Oh, Mamie!" Eric said disgustedly. "If we had done that, we would have frozen solid! They wouldn't have found us until next July! As it was we almost froze to death during the last part, when the blizzard hit and we spent hours going down the last, easy slopes. It was lucky we weren't still up at the top when that happened, or we could never have gotten out.

"I'll never forget that run," Eric concluded. "I think we really must have broken all previous records for speed, until the blizzard caught us. I'm sure I couldn't do it again, and I would never have believed that Alex could ski like that!"

"Neither would I," said Alex, "but it shows that you never know what a person can do until he's given sufficient incentive."

"It was getting dark by the time we finally got down," Eric went on, not intending to leave out any part of what was, after all, a good story, "and we saw the lights of a café through the snowstorm, just on the other side of a road. We started across, but I was so exhausted, or dazed, or whatever, that I didn't even realize until the last minute that one of those huge snowplows was looming up at me out of the storm. I just stood there like an idiot, and I didn't have enough energy left to move."

"Obviously you did move, though," his father interjected dryly.

"No, actually Alex somehow pushed me out of the way," Eric confessed.

"It's not just exhaustion that makes you so apathetic," Alex explained. "It's also lack of adrenaline. You had probably used up a year's supply long before we got to the road. I felt the same way. I said to myself. There's my sister's precious firstborn son about to be crushed by a huge truck. Do I care? Not really. But then I thought, Maybe I'll throw myself over there and push him out of the way anyway, just for the exercise."

"Oh, Alex!" Eric protested, to general laughter.

"But the funniest part," Eric recalled, "was when we staggered into the café, half frozen and covered with snow, and it turned out to be a fancy bar full of dressed-up people. Remember, Alex? We both ordered hot chocolate, and after the waitress left, I asked you if you didn't want something stronger. You said you did, but you didn't think they would give it to you there. When I asked you what you had in mind, you said, 'A blood transfusion, type B positive.' That struck me as very funny, at the time."

"I guess that was excusable, under the circumstances," Alex told him.

"Then that blond American woman with all the diamonds went around asking everybody if they spoke English, and when she got to you and you said yes, she wanted you to tell the bartender exactly how to mix her drink. And everybody came and stood around us, arguing over our heads about how much of this or that to put in, and you looked like you were about to die and I guess I did, too, and then we looked at each other and started laughing so hard they thought we were crazy!"

"A fascinating story!" Grisha exclaimed. "What is the moral of this story, do you think?" he asked Eric.

"The moral is," Eric answered quite logically, "that foreigners in France should drink what the French drink, and if they want their drinks mixed a special way they should learn French, and not pester people who have just practically gotten themselves killed!"

"What do you say to that?" Grisha turned to Alex. "I think the boy has a point."

"He has a point," Alex agreed. "But I think the moral is that you may get yourself killed or not, as you please, but either way, don't expect the world to stop and notice."

"People are too busy with their own affairs," Grisha

agreed. "That's human nature, Sasha. You can't expect too much of it."

He shook his head. "Sometimes, though, I wonder how otherwise decent people can pay no attention even to the harm they themselves do. There was an article in the paper today about a woman in Reims who accused a man of robbery, and had him arrested. She was so anxious to have someone arrested that she identified the first man she saw. The poor fellow was in the hospital when the crime was committed. How can anyone thoughtlessly make such an accusation? He might have sat in jail for years."

It occurred to Alex that he had once been guilty of making a similarly thoughtless accusation. Grisha's remarks reminded him what it was about the long-ago incident with the school bully that had bothered him afterward. He remembered why Sani had been ready to kill him. The toady, Andräs, had incited him to it.

"Hit him, Sani! Hit him again!" Andräs had yelled. "He's the one who told on you!"

"Told what, to whom?" Alex had asked distractedly, more concerned with the movements of the heavy plank that Sani had already tried to bring down on his head. Then some trace of desperation in Andräs' expression, and uncertainty in Sani's, inspired him to say, "You told on him yourself, you little weasel!" Andräs had taken off like lightning, and Sani had dropped the plank to chase him.

He knew at the time that he had behaved badly. Under the stress of the moment he had blurted out an accusation that was only a guess and the following day Andräs had appeared at school with a black eye and a broken arm. The fact that they were no doubt well deserved may have excused Sani, but didn't make his own role any more admirable.

Hearing about the irresponsible woman in Reims wouldn't have been enough to resurrect such an ancient memory if he hadn't partially recalled the incident more recently. It wasn't so long ago that Nina, the woman who used to be Elisha Tal's technician, had reminded him of sadistic little Andräs. What had become of him? Under the influence of the good dinner and the warm surroundings, Alex was able to hope that Andräs had remembered the lesson learned from that early experience longer than he himself had, and had grown up to be a fine man.

The evening drew to a close, but before Sylvie left it was arranged that Eva and Alex would go to an exhibition at the Bibliothèque Nationale in the morning, then meet Sylvie at lunchtime, and that she and Alex would go on to the concert at La Madeleine.

After Eva and the boys had done the washing up and everyone had left, Alex's mother couldn't resist saying, "Why couldn't you have married Sylvie, Alex? You get along so well together."

"Yes, mother, but we don't love each other," Alex replied. It was not the first time his mother had voiced this thought.

"And you do love that red-headed witch?" she went on. "I'll never forgive her for what she did to you, and especially for not even bothering to tell me! If she had at least called me, I would have come immediately! I can never forget that you were alone in the hospital for weeks, and I didn't even know about it!"

"Please stop worrying about it, Mother," Alex said. "It was years ago. Anyway, there was nothing you could have done, and it wasn't that bad."

"I'm sure you just say that to make me feel better," his mother maintained.

"No, honestly. The food was even good. It was a nice vacation, really." Simone remained unconvinced, but she smiled, taking some comfort from his assurances.

In the morning Eva met him at the national library, where they both wanted to see the exhibit of Cretan antiquities. Alex was very interested in ancient history, and especially in the decipherment of ancient scripts. They lingered over a model of the Phaistos disk, that clay platter covered with strange heiroglyphs that no one had been able to understand as yet.

"I tried my hand at deciphering this once," he told her. "I spent most of a rainy week in a tent on it, during one stint in the reserves."

"And did you get anywhere?" she asked.

"No," he answered. "I could tell that it's in rhyme, and I assume it's a hymn to a god or goddess representing the sun or the moon, but I couldn't get much more out of it."

"What a way to spend a week!" Eva exclaimed.

"I like to understand things," her brother explained. "It's one of life's greatest pleasures."

"Even greater than women?" she asked.

"Ouf! Women!" he responded in the same bantering tone, with a nice imitation of the Gallic shrug and switching from Hungarian to French. "Women come and women go, but once you understand something, you know it."

Afterward they spent an hour or so over coffee with Sylvie, before Eva went home to prepare the dinner for Alex's last evening in Paris, and Sylvie and Alex went on to the Madeleine Church for the Sunday afternoon concert.

They found places about halfway back in the cavernous stone interior and settled down for the first part of the program, three short pieces of sacred music played on the church's powerful organ.

The second part of the program was a full-dress presentation of Bach's Magnificat. The audience sat in rapt attention as the glorious choral music washed over it. One should be careful of this kind of music, Alex thought; it churned up confusing emotions that would remain unresolved when the music ended.

During the Misericordia, when Sylvie suddenly grasped his hand and he saw that tears were streaming down her cheeks, Alex felt—he didn't know what he felt.

CHAPTER 17

It was early evening when Alex disembarked at Lod airport near Tel Aviv. He went through the "nothing to declare" line with his single small suitcase without being stopped. Customs agents never showed any interest in him. He didn't know whether this should be taken as a compliment or an insult, but it was convenient.

He walked out of the terminal into the balmy evening, expecting to look for one of the seven-passenger taxis that would make the trip to Jerusalem as soon as all the seats were filled. He had almost walked right by without seeing them when Daniel ran over, calling out excitedly, and threw his arms around him. The surging crowd had prevented him from noticing Varda, who was usually hard to miss because of her height and her spectacular hair.

Her paintings these days often had more to do with color than with form, and her sense of color was expressed no less in the clothes she wore, which always complemented her dark red hair and milk-white skin. She disliked her coloring, and considered it a not-so-minor tragedy that her complexion made it esthetically sinful to wear the whites and beiges she loved. This evening she was dressed in inky blue, and a pin in the form of a gauzy, pale yellow butterfly nestled on her blouse, just beneath the heavy burnished waves that cascaded over her shoulders.

He hugged the bright-headed boy, and kissed Varda on the cheek. "What a wonderful surprise!" he said to Daniel, and to Varda, "I didn't expect you to meet me."

"Why not?" she replied archly. "I'm your wife, aren't I?"

In a manner of speaking, he could have answered, but there was no point in it.

"Actually," she continued, "I'm invited to a party in Herzelia. It's a reception for a wonderful young artist from Milan, and I promised to be there to help out, since I speak some Italian." Alex looked at her in surprise. This was news to him. But now came the point. "So I thought you could just drive me over there from the airport, and then you could take Daniel home with you. If there's no one to get a ride with back to Jerusalem afterward, I'll just stay over with somebody in Tel Aviv. Isn't that a good idea? This way you don't have to wait for a taxi, and I don't have to disappoint my friends."

It was an extremely inconsiderate request, since Herzelia and Jerusalem were in opposite directions. But after a quick self-inspection, Alex agreed. Though still biologically on U.S. time, he felt reasonably wide awake for the moment, and he would be rewarded for the long drive by being spared an evening of Varda's chatter. He had no patience for it when he was tired.

The next morning he was at the lab early. There was a paper to be rewritten and a report to a funding agency to send out by the end of the month. Unfortunately plunging into the work didn't prevent him from noticing how depressing it was to come home, and how quickly the effect of the few days in Paris dissipated. It was a good thing that Daniel was growing up, because he was no longer sure that he could keep up this mode of existence indefinitely.

He emptied a drawer onto his desk, looking for an earlier version of the paper he was rewriting. There was a lot of stuff that could be recycled as scratch paper, forgotten early drafts of papers that had already come out. He obviously hadn't cleaned out this drawer in a long time.

Among the outdated material there was even a draft of the original article on protein phosphorylation. This was a very early draft, he saw. It looked like the version he had given to Ilan Falk, the one Ilan hadn't liked and never found the time to work on. He couldn't understand why he still had it, unless it was Ilan's copy that he had shoved into the drawer when Ilan returned it and not needed since.

There were some loose pages that might belong to another paper, and he pulled them out to make sure that he didn't need them before throwing the whole thing onto the discard pile. He stared at the first of these, stunned to see that his glib invention of two years ago was a reality—it was a draft of a letter from Ilan Falk to the Landon Prize Committee, informing them that Elisha Tal had won the prize for forged results, and demanding that this fact be publicized immediately and the prize withdrawn.

He had to read the second page twice before its meaning sank in. It was another letter from Ilan, this one to the president of the university, in regard to Nina Ben Neriah.

She had participated in the falsification of results in the laboratory of Professor Elisha Tal, Ilan claimed. He demanded that proceedings to revoke her tenure and fire her be started at once.

Alex was still working at his desk at six o'clock, when Micky came in to say hello.

"What's on your mind?" he asked, realizing that Alex wasn't interested in discussing his trip. Wordlessly, Alex handed him the two letters. Micky's amazed expression would have seemed funnier if Alex hadn't known that his own expression when he first came across those two pages must have been exactly the same.

"I called Miriam Tal and asked her whether she had known that Nina was involved in the supposed forgery in Elisha's lab," Alex reported. "She had. It was Nina who went to Miriam with the story and made her promise not to tell anyone where she got the information. But now that it doesn't matter anymore, and since I knew anyway that Nina was involved, she was willing to tell me about it. She had finally also told Ilan that the information came from Nina. He had last-minute doubts about accusing Elisha without checking the information personally, so she had to send him to Nina."

"But why did Nina want to cause all that trouble? And why bring Miriam into it?" Micky asked, bewildered by this new development.

"I don't know why she wanted to do it," Alex replied, "but she wanted Miriam to be the one to publicize the story so that her own name wouldn't come up."

"This is getting very complicated," Micky commented, "for something that's supposed to be over and done with. I would give a lot to know what actually happened." Alex nodded his agreement.

"You'll have to talk to Nina," Micky said authoritatively. "I'm sure you can charm the information out of her."

"I don't think so," Alex said.

"Come on, settle this for us! Kiss her hand, or whatever it is Hungarians do."

"You're stepping onto dangerous ground," Alex warned without menace.

"This is important!" Micky insisted.

"Charm her yourself, if the idea appeals to you!" Alex said with uncharacteristic sharpness.

"I'm no good at that kind of thing," Micky protested.

"Well, neither am I," Alex responded.

Their next conversation was a few days later, when Alex went into Micky's office to ask him a question. Micky had a phenomenal memory. Alex was sure that he would remember who it was who had done a particular piece of work that he wanted to mention in his next lecture.

Of course Micky remembered the name. After he had provided the information, he said, "I don't suppose you've tried to talk to Nina?"

"No," Alex replied shortly.

Micky nodded. "I'm not going to pester you about it. I know exactly how you feel.

"This business about the letters has kept me up at night. I've been thinking of how Elisha was suddenly gone, without anyone having a chance to ask any questions. I thought that it wasn't fair to insist that you be the one to find out what actually happened, so yesterday I went looking for Nina myself."

"And?" Alex prompted.

"You were right. It's a hard thing to do. I found her down in the stockroom, checking the supplies for the student labs. Did you know that she was working there now?"

Alex shook his head.

"I'm glad you weren't there to see me! I tracked her down, and when I saw her, I said, 'Nina! I didn't know you were working here!' " Micky imitated the guileless expression he had assumed to make Nina think that he had come across her by happenstance. The trouble was, Micky's ordinary expression was so guileless that when it was exaggerated he looked like an idiot.

"Don't laugh," he said reproachfully. "I've already admitted that I made a mess of it. She just gave me a dirty look. I couldn't think of anything else to say. That was it."

CHAPTER 18

He had been home for a month when Shosh appeared in his office doorway.

"Hello, Alex," she said, smiling shyly.

It took him a moment to recover the power of speech.

"Hello!" he said. "Are you back in Jerusalem now?"

"No," she said. "We're living in Tel Aviv. I came in for the day, to take care of some things. And to see some people. I wanted—" She stopped, seeming not to know how to continue.

"How is Avi?" Alex asked.

"He's better," she said. They looked at each other silently, and in another moment she was gone.

It was inexpressibly sad to exchange a few meaningless phrases with Shosh in this way, but he was forced to put it out of his mind almost at once, because he was due in the lab to run an experiment with Nureet, a new master's student. This was an experiment he had suggested to Nureet and helped her to plan. They were going to share the work this first time, for two reasons; it would be much easier with two pairs of hands, and the experiment involved radioactive material that he would show her how to handle.

Several aspects of a radioactively labeled bacterial cell culture would be measured at the same time. Every five minutes, during the course of an hour, two sets of samples were to be taken from each of four cultures and treatment of each of them begun. It demanded total concentration because they had to work fast, and because the radioactive material was^{32}p, a high-energy beta-ray emitter.

He shielded the radioactive tubes and flasks with plexiglass screens and left the Geiger counter on, so that its frantic beeping would remind Nureet of his instruction to stay out of range until she had to approach the samples, and to handle them as little as possible.

That night he went to sleep on the couch in the small room he used as a study, as he did more and more often. He woke only a few hours later, his heart pounding and his mouth dry. In his dream, a woman appeared and lay down in the bed beside him. It was Shosh, he thought at first, although the face was indistinct. No, he realized, it wasn't Shosh. He knew, though, that possession of this unknown woman would bring him the peace and happiness that were absent from his life.

But it seemed that peace and happiness were not to be his lot even in dreams. He gathered the unknown woman in a fierce embrace, but barely had time to feel the ecstasy that flooded through him at the first touch of her lips when she disappeared, to be replaced by a vindictive Elisha Tal who was trying to drive a tank over him and crush him to death. It was the sharp pain in his chest that woke him.

He lay motionless for a few minutes, waiting for the emotional turmoil to subside and for his breathing to return to normal, then got up and turned on the light. He spent the rest of the night reading, since there was no possibility of falling asleep again. Finally he decided to shower and go to work.

It was still too early to wake Daniel, and he sat at the kitchen table drinking instant coffee and trying to exorcise the night's images from his mind. Varda didn't have a fixed schedule and didn't usually appear before he left in the morning, but like a cat that instinctively gravitates to where it's least wanted, she came in this morning, brushing unruly red tresses out of her eyes, and dropped into the chair opposite.

"Did I tell you that the American art dealer telephoned? You know, the one who came the other day to look at my work, and hurt her ankle?" she began. "She's decided to take two paintings back with her on consignment. She's sure they'll sell for a lot of money. But the main thing is, she's going to arrange a show for me in New York. Isn't that fantastic?"

Alex agreed that it was wonderful.

Looking at him for the first time, she continued, "You look tired, Alex. There are dark circles under your eyes. You shouldn't sleep on that couch; you can't get a good night's rest there. And I don't like it when you don't come to bed."

The trouble was that Alex generally found it harder to get a good night's rest in the bed with Varda. The combined effect of physical attraction and tightly reined emotion was far from soothing, and perhaps worst of all were the times when he woke in the morning to find her twined around him with her cheek resting on his chest, just as if there were some feeling between them.

"I'm so excited about it," she was saying. "She was very enthusiastic, especially about the studies in red, you know the ones, you liked them, too. The problem is that she wants me to do more like them, and of course I can't paint to order. I put a lot of myself into those canvases, they didn't just happen. You can't know what it's like, but believe me it isn't easy. Oh, Alex, be nice and make me a cup of coffee, too, will you?"

The instant coffee and kettle were at Varda's elbow, and as Alex didn't move she stood up to make her own coffee, still talking.

"How will you like being married to a famous artist? I know the answer to that! You'll pretend that it isn't important, but you'll love it! I understand you so well."

Jézus, Mária! Alex exclaimed mentally. There was no reason why she shouldn't understand him, he thought, since there was nothing unusual or complicated about him. But even an amoeba couldn't be understood without giving a moment's thought to the creature. There was one advantage in Varda's failure to devote that moment to understanding him. It meant that there was no need for him to dissemble, since she could be counted on not to notice any but the most extreme behavioral aberrations.

He remained slumped in his chair without responding, gazing at her over his coffee cup and deciding, on considering the way she looked in her thin white pajamas, that she was wrong to think that white didn't suit her. On the contrary, the lack of distinction between the cloth and her milky skin gave her a look of naked vulnerability that was very appealing.

"Did I mention that she asked about you?" Varda continued the one-sided conversation. "Well, she did. She must have told me ten times how wonderful you are."

The art dealer was a clumsy, overweight, middle-aged woman with the poor sense to wear high-heeled shoes, and she had tripped and fallen heavily on the stairs as she left their apartment. Alex was accompanying her out to wait for her cab, but was behind her on the stairs and unable to prevent the fall.

When he helped her to her feet, they realized that she couldn't put her weight on her left leg. He felt it for signs of broken bones, as he had learned to do in the army, and decided that it was probably just a bad sprain. Still, someone would have to take her to the emergency room to have it x-rayed and bandaged.

The woman was Varda's guest and he had only met her by chance, because she was still there enthusing about Varda's work when he came home. It would have been reasonable for Varda to take her, but she hadn't offered and he didn't want to argue about it in the woman's presence. As it was her distress seemed to be due in equal parts to her hurt leg and to the thought that she was causing bother. So he didn't mention that it was late and he was tired, but assured her that it was no trouble and took her first to the emergency room and then back to her hotel, where he supported her as she hobbled to her room.

"You're too nice to people, Alex," Varda said. "You let everybody take advantage of you."

Alex lowered his eyes to his cup, so that only the dark lashes were visible. He froze as a flood of images poured into his mind in response to those phrases, in this context.

As clearly as if it had been yesterday, he saw himself in the hospital bed between operations, when every time they would stitch something up, something else would come apart, when days and nights ran into each other and none of the pills or injections could alleviate the constant pain. A procession of strange faces had leaned over him during those days, doctors and nurses, blond and brunette, young and old.

Sometimes he grasped a hand that was held out to him in kindness, but he knew that only one hand and only one face could give him the strength he needed. And she didn't come.

He wondered that years later those images still came so readily to mind. They would probably be with him until the day he died. You couldn't say that Varda was "too nice to people," and he had learned to his sorrow how hard it was to take advantage of her.

He fled to the lab. He had to prepare for the lecture on bacterial genetics he was supposed to give that afternoon, but he often caught himself reading the same sentence over and over as his mind drifted uncontrollably back to the troubling dream of the previous night. Before he realized it, it was time to go to the classroom. He had forgotten to eat lunch.

After the lecture—not one of his best—there was only one more thing he had to do before going home, and that was to distill phenol. The students would need it in the morning to complete their preparation of DNA. In order not to damage the DNA the reagent had to be pure, but it oxidized readily and the commercial product generally wasn't clean enough to use.

Since Arik had completed his research and stopped working in the lab, there was no one to undertake this dirty job. They weren't shirkers. They just seemed to be afraid of distillation, even though it was a standard technique taught in all organic chemistry courses. He kept meaning to give them a practice session in the distillation of phenol, but until he got around to it he would have to do it himself.

He had to borrow the distillation apparatus, and it was evening before he was able to start. The intricate blown-glass pieces used in distillation are very expensive, so he was extremely careful with the borrowed equipment, setting the round-bottomed flask in the contoured heating pad and attaching the special thermometer, condenser, and receiving flask, all within the ventilated hood that would prevent the escape of poisonous fumes.

It began well enough, the temperature in the neck of the round-bottomed flask quickly reaching 100 degrees Centigrade, and he discarded the water or whatever it was that boiled off at that temperature. Then something went wrong, and he couldn't get the temperature up to the 160 degrees Centigrade required to boil phenol. Finally he tried turning off the ventilation, and the temperature shot up immediately. Unfortunately the escape of fumes into the room became catastrophic at the same time.

He couldn't escape for more than a few minutes at a time, since it was impossible to leave this witch's cauldron unattended, and in any case the fumes immediately spread into the corridor also. Luckily there were few people left in the other labs, and no one came to complain. He opened all the windows and tried to relieve his burning throat by inhaling the fresh evening air.

He was stretched out on the wooden chair near the window with his eyes closed, wondering whether it was the previous restless night or the acrid fumes that made his head swim and feeling like one of the denizens of the first circle of hell. A sudden burst of coughing nearby made him open his eyes to see Nureet standing in front of him.

"Excuse me," she apologized. "I didn't want to bother you."

"You're not bothering me," he said. "But what are you doing here?"

"I have some questions about the experiment we did," she said. "I heard you say you would take care of the phenol this evening, and I thought . . . Could we go over it now?"

"Forgive me," Alex told her. "This isn't a good time." Nureet was a timid girl, and seeing her hurt expression, he forced himself to smile and elaborate.

"I'm tired," he explained. "And I don't think that breathing phenol instead of oxygen has improved my powers of concentration. Will you have time to talk to me after class tomorrow?"

She acceded with a shy smile, but made no move to leave. "I could make you a cup of coffee," she said tentatively.

"On no, thank you," Alex told her. "You go home. There's no need for both of us to be asphyxiated."

It would be silly for Nureet to stay in this place when she didn't have to; her turn to suffer would come soon enough. But maybe the coffee was a good idea? No, he decided. Anything he ate or drank now would taste like phenol.

It was hard not to see the deadly miasma that enveloped him as a metaphor for the circumstances of his life, but he avoided the thought with a conscious effort. By refusing to admit to himself that he was trying to do something that was beyond his capability, he held on to the possibility that he would be able to do it after all.

He set his sights on the modest goal of solving the immediate problem; in no more than an hour, with any luck, he would be able to shower the phenol out of his skin and hair and drink a cup of coffee that would taste like coffee.

CHAPTER 19

Alex was almost ready to leave his office one evening a few days later when Nina came in and planted herself in front of his desk. She was rather elegantly dressed in a purple sweater and a flowing black skirt and high boots. A thin silver chain swung across her breasts as she tossed the long black hair out of her eyes.

Was Alex aware, she asked, of the conspiracy to take her job away? She had been sure that he wasn't. She hadn't gotten along in the various labs they had sent her to work in after Elisha died, that was true, but none of it was her fault; one professor was old and senile, another young and arrogant, and in the third laboratory, the students had forced her out because she wouldn't let them take advantage of her or cooperate in their intrigues.

Now the current department chairman, who had been against her from the beginning, was threatening to have her fired by the university if she couldn't find herself a lab to settle down in right away. If that happened, she would have to start all over again acquiring job security and pension rights with some other employer. And with Elisha gone, she had no one to give her a recommendation. She wasn't going to tell Alex her age, but she was sure it was greater than he thought; it would be hard for her to recover from the financial damage they would be doing her, not to mention the humiliation and loss of reputation.

Nina was one of the tenured technicians who received their salaries from the university; each faculty member, from the rank of senior lecturer, was entitled to one such technician in his lab, and they were moved around as positions became available. Each head of a laboratory could also, of course, hire additional technical help if he had enough grant money to allow it.

"You could take me on as your technician," she concluded. "I know it would work out beautifully. You have the right to a technician now, but you don't have anyone yet, and we've always gotten along well."

"I don't think it would work out," Alex said, knowing it was important to make himself clear. "I'm sorry. I'm not going to do it."

She digested his reply in silence for a moment. "So you're just like the others, after all," she said finally. Then, in a more conciliatory tone, "Well, if you aren't going to save my neck, will you at least give me a lift home? My old junk heap is in the garage."

"All right," he said, and they left the building together. After they had driven for a few minutes without speaking, she suddenly said, "Could we stop for something to drink before you take me home? I don't want to spend all evening by myself, brooding in an empty apartment." That was the point at which he would have demurred if he hadn't had an ulterior motive for staying with Nina.

She wanted to go to the café at the cinema club. It was just across the road from the Sultan's Pool and before one came to Yemin Moshe, not too far past where she lived in Rehavia. The new stone building was set into the hillside. After dark, as now, the illuminated walls of the Old City glowed high above, on the other side of the valley.

"Everybody comes here," she said with satisfaction as they seated themselves at a table in the café.

"I love old French movies, don't you?" she asked. The posters they had passed on their way into the café advertised a festival of French movies from the fifties and sixties.

He ordered espresso, and she asked for white wine. She chatted on, displaying her familiarity with French cinema, with only occasional brief replies from Alex.

This is a typical conversation between two people who have nothing to say to each other, he thought, wishing that he could be somewhere else. He reminded himself that while facing a woman he disliked across a café table under more-or-less false pretenses wasn't pleasant, there were worse punishments.

In any case he had no choice, since he had set the trap that resulted in Elisha's death. As long as anything about the events of that time remained unclear, it was possible that he had missed or misunderstood something, and that he had made the wrong decision. He had to know. Micky had been right at that; if Nina hadn't come to him, sooner or later he would have had to take the initiative and go to her.

"I see that you aren't very interested in French cinema," she observed finally. "Don't worry about it. I have the ad–

vantage of knowing some French, but of course it's hard to enjoy French movies if you have to follow the plot by reading the Hebrew subtitles."

Since Alex had barely listened to her remarks, he didn't know what she was talking about. Why on earth would he want to follow a French movie by reading the Hebrew subtitles? This was useless, he decided, and was beginning to cause him acute suffering. He would prefer spending the entire night looking for answers at the lab bench to spending half an hour like this, trapped in a phony conversation and wondering how to extract information from Nina.

"I didn't bring you here to pester you," she said, "but I really think you're making a mistake by not giving me a job in your lab. I have a very good background in science. I almost got my Ph.D.; I did everything but the thesis." This was like saying, I almost got my pilot's license, I did everything except actually fly a plane. But at least she now had his full attention.

"And I can be very helpful on a research project," she went on. "I contributed a lot in Elisha's lab."

"But then you accused him of faking results," Alex said.

Nina was startled out of her composure. "So Miriam told you, too!" she said. "That was only after extreme provocation. He had dropped me and taken up with that little nitwit Orli. I had to make him pay for that."

"And you went to Miriam so that your name would stay out of it."

"Yes. I went to her, and I suggested that she tell Ilan. Elisha and I knew how jealous Ilan was when we won the prize, so I knew he would be sure to make use of the information. I thought the Landon committee would be much more likely to take an accusation like that seriously if it came from another professor. But I didn't want Ilan to know the information came from me. If Elisha had ever guessed that I was the one . . ." He might have tried to kill you, instead of Miriam, Alex finished the sentence mentally.

They had finished their drinks. He insisted on paying for both of them, as if that would make up for not having enjoyed her company, and took her home.

"I was telling the truth about the doctored results," she said as he pulled up to the curb in front of the building she pointed out, "but I suppose you'd like to see for yourself." Alex admitted that he would. "Come on up, then," she said, almost defiantly, "and I'll show you."

She led him into a small but pretty room with a colorful carpet and embroidered pillows scattered on the couch and chairs. Polished copper containers of the type sold in the bazaar, some of them filled with dried grasses or flowers, stood on the floor and on several small tables.

Inviting him to sit down on the couch, she asked whether he would like to drink a glass of cognac while she looked for the notebook that she had removed from Elisha's lab two years ago. She had a really good bottle from France. Although he declined, she put the glass of dark amber-colored liquid in his hand anyway before disappearing into another room.

One sip was enough to send a beautiful warmth diffusing through his body. A glass of this would undoubtedly bring nirvana. Nirvana didn't interest him at the moment. He left the glass on the table and got up to wander impatiently around the room.

There was little more to be seen here, only a few small charcoal sketches on the walls and one book, by Shai Agnon, lying on a table. He was Israel's only Nobel Prize–winning author, but Alex had never read any of his work. It was considered hard going even for those who had gone to school in Israel, and he had accepted the judgment that it would be beyond his comprehension.

When Nina reappeared with the black hardcover notebook he returned to sit beside her on the couch. The pages were peppered with glued-in strips similar to those of an electrocardiogram. These were graphs representing the output of the column chromatography by which their protein had been separated from contaminating proteins. Alex didn't know one peak on these graphs from another, and he was afraid that studying this notebook would leave him no wiser. But the matter turned out to be surprisingly simple.

"It was easy to fool everybody," Nina explained, "because we were almost there anyway. So were two other labs. Why let someone else get all the credit when we were so close to complete purification, and knew exactly how it was going to turn out?

"Do you see this graph?" she continued. "If you look closely, you can see that there was a shoulder on the main peak, but it's been erased. Look at this photo of a polyacrylamide gel. There seems to be only one protein here, at thirty-eight megadaltons. But now look at this one." She pulled another photograph out of an envelope inserted between two pages of the notebook. A detailed comparison showed it to be the same gel. Only there was a heavy smear of contaminating material surrounding the thirty-eight megadalton band. The first photo had been retouched.

"And the specific activity," she went on. "Anyone could guess it was going to be somewhere around two hundred thousand international units per milligram. It was easy to adjust the numbers in the mouse assay to show that."

She showed him a table listing increasing concentrations of purified protein in the left-hand column and on the right, increasing red-blood-cell counts. The numbers were entered clearly in black ink, and a graph of the data on the facing page, an almost perfect straight line, gave the resulting specific activity; 218,000 international units per milligram.

"This is your notebook, isn't it?" Alex asked. "Did Elisha ever see the original data?"

"That's what Ilan asked me," she said. "I told him that it was Elisha who made all the changes in the data, but he didn't believe me. He was going to confront Elisha and find out who was responsible; Elisha, me, or both of us together."

"He would have found out that it was you," Alex stated.

"There was no reason for me to do it! Elisha was the one who was determined to get the prize."

"Maybe you did it for him, then," Alex guessed.

"Elisha did it himself," she insisted.

"You said that this is your notebook," he reminded her.

"Well?"

"All the entries are in the same black ink, and the same handwriting—"

"He told me what to write! Elisha was no fool. He knew better than to write in my notebook."

"—except this." He pointed to a faint green design next to the too-perfect table. It seemed to have been made by a malfunctioning ballpoint pen, but on close inspection it was definitely a question mark, a large, sprawling one in an entirely different style than that of the neat lettering.

"I never saw that before! I have no idea how it got there!" Nina protested.

"I do," Alex replied. "Elisha looked over the data in your notebook, and when he got to this table he couldn't help realizing that it was too good to be true. Didn't he ever ask you about it?"

Nina didn't reply for a moment. "No," she said finally.

"So when Ilan said that he would go to Elisha—"

"I couldn't let him do that! I had only done it to help, but by this time—God knows what Elisha would have done to me if he had found out! He really had a terrible temper." Judging by the tone in which she said this, it had been one of the things she admired about him.

"But I thought of a way to solve the problem," she said, sounding pleased with herself. "I simply told him that Ilan was about to write to the committee, accusing him of faking results."

"So he knew about it even before Miriam told him," Alex stated.

"No, she got to him first. By the time I talked to him,

he was already furious at both of them, and that made it easier. That same day we planned how he was going to get rid of Ilan.

"It doesn't matter now if I tell you that Ilan's death was no accident. I found out for Elisha when Ilan was going to be around the lab, and he sneaked in and turned the gas on. Everyone knew that idiot always smoked his cigars while he was working!

"But barely one month later, Elisha was dead himself," she continued thoughtfully. "There was something very odd about that. What was he doing in your lab? He wasn't by any chance trying to make trouble for you when he died, was he?"

"You could put it that way," Alex said.

"But instead you killed him!"

"No," he said, but she was gone. She had stood up abruptly and run into what appeared to be the kitchen. He barely had time to wonder what she was doing when she returned, more slowly, to plant herself aggressively in front of him, her chin thrust forward and her hands behind her back.

"You're all the same, aren't you?" she said bitterly. "You don't appreciate real intelligence and culture in a woman. Or even total dedication. As soon as some little dope bats her eyelashes at you and tells you you're wonderful, she can do whatever she likes with you!"

"I always thought, in spite of everything, that one day I would get Elisha back. But then he died. Because of you.

"Now you're going to let them throw me out of my job.

You don't even think I'm worth spending a few hours with! You only came here to find out whether I faked the data. Well, a lab notebook isn't the only thing I can show you!" She brought her right hand out from behind her, and the blade of the knife flashed in the lamplight.

He stood up slowly, as if to avoid startling a wild animal, and faced her with the couch at his back.

"I see I've suddenly become more interesting," she said sarcastically. "Now you're going to say, 'Please, Nina, put the knife away. Come and sit back down beside me and we'll talk about this.' "

He stood perfectly still and didn't say a word.

"That would be a dangerous move on my part," she resumed, "since you're stronger than I am. But I might take the chance. If you asked me very nicely. Well?"

He still hadn't moved. The situation was so novel and surprising that he had no idea what to do. He only knew that he didn't feel like trying to wheedle the knife away from Nina.

"You think all you have to do is stand there and look at me," she said furiously, "and I'll collapse in a heap! You think you're God's gift to the world! Well, you don't impress me. The world is full of people who are worth ten of you!"

"I know," he said.

"And Elisha was one of them!"

"Well—" he said.

"Somebody has to pay for ruining my life," she went on stubbornly, taking a tentative step toward him with the knife held out in front of her, "and it may as well be you."

"I don't deny that I'm partly responsible for Elisha's death," he said reasonably, ignoring for the moment the blade pointed in the general direction of his heart, "but it was accidental—and he was trying to kill me! But how about you? If you hadn't fed him fake results and then tried to ruin him with them he would still be alive, and you would still be working with him."

"This isn't very clever of you," she said, taking another step toward him so that the tip of the knife separated a large red square on his checked shirt from a gray one, and the cold point pricked his skin through the T-shirt underneath. "Not under the circumstances."

He was afraid to take a deep breath, in case it might force the blade into his diaphragm. He was also afraid to make any move to take the knife from her, for the same reason. He was wondering himself, even as he spoke, about the wisdom of confronting Nina with unpleasant truths in their present relative positions.

"He might never have murdered anyone, if not for you," he said. "You manipulated him into killing Ilan and helped him do it. Because of you, he nearly killed Miriam.

"I didn't give a damn who first isolated the protein, but someone with more public spirit might have found out about the fraud. Elisha would have had to kill him, too. You could have been responsible for a whole string of murders. Do you really think other people are to blame for all your troubles?"

The knife didn't shift, or even quiver. Her only response was an appraising look that seemed to reflect indecision over where she would hang his mounted head.

"Killing me won't help you," he concluded, "and anyway you know I'm not going to let you do it."

"We'll see, won't we?" she said, with the crooked smile he remembered, apparently anticipating something nasty that she was going to enjoy very much. "But first you're going to jump for me. Like a scared rabbit."

She flashed the blade toward his face, and he leaned back instinctively. Where had he heard that phrase before? Elisha had said it to him. He had come between an ideally matched couple.

She was looking intently at a point near his right ear, evidently intending to make her next feint in that direction, but had barely managed to raise the knife a little higher in preparation when he grasped her wrist. She was surprisingly strong and stubborn, but she couldn't prevent him from removing the hilt from her grip with his other hand. He was relieved to see that he hadn't been scratched; if he had given her the satisfaction of drawing blood he couldn't have forgiven himself.

The hand had been quicker not than the eye, but than the mind; she didn't seem to understand how the knife that had been in her hand a moment before was now in his.

"I'm taking this with me," he said as he turned to go. "You can buy yourself another one for the next occasion."

"If you try to make trouble for me," she said to his back, "I'll say you were trying to rape me!"

When he entered his apartment he found Varda and Daniel in the living room, Daniel in pajamas.

"It's almost nine thirty!" Varda said accusingly. "Where

have you been? You said you would be home early, so Daniel refused to go to bed until you came home!"

"I'm sorry," he apologized. "I didn't realize you were waiting for me."

"I suppose you got tied up, as usual, with those bottles and test tubes you find so fascinating."

"No," he replied. "I was all through with the bottles and test tubes, but I had a chance to talk to someone who had some information I wanted." It is a serious drawback of the Hebrew language that there is no neuter word for "someone," so it was clear that he had spent the evening with a female.

"It was very inconsiderate," Varda went on, obviously annoyed. "I might have made plans to go out, and I would have been stuck here with Daniel."

"But you didn't!" Daniel said, jumping up. "You weren't planning to go anywhere. Anyway, you know I'm not afraid to stay by myself."

"He gets more and more like you every day," Varda said angrily. "And the two of you gang up on me."

"Please," Alex said, "whatever complaints you may have about me, don't take them out on Daniel." He moved closer to Daniel, but the boy moved away. His look said as clearly as words, I don't need help with this.

Alex smiled and quickly changed the subject. "Is there any bread in the house?" he asked.

"I brought some rolls from the corner grocery this afternoon," Daniel told him. "And there's salami and tomatoes in the refrigerator. We had sandwiches."

"Good," Alex said. "I'm starved." He went toward the kitchen and Daniel followed him.

"You must have worked up an appetite, getting that information from your *someone!*" Varda called after him from the living room. Alex didn't answer.

"I'm going out after all," she added. Without waiting for a response from the kitchen, she left, slamming the door.

Daniel made instant coffee for Alex and sat across from him while he ate.

"What sort of information did you want from that woman, Daddy?" he asked. "Was it something to do with your research?"

"No," Alex explained. "It was something to do with some of the people at work."

"But it was important?"

"It was important to me, because I did something a while ago that—that changed those people's lives. And that made me feel responsible to see it through to the end."

"Did you run into something sharp?" Daniel asked. "There's a rip in your shirt."

"I wouldn't be surprised," Alex replied without looking down.

"Do you think a person always has to finish everything he starts?" the boy asked. "You were the one who said that it was all right to quit when Shiri started to feel sick while we were hiking. You said that she didn't have to climb all the way to the top of the hill just because she had started out—that wasn't a good reason for doing something."

"That was different," Alex explained. "That didn't affect

anyone except herself. But if you do something that affects other people, you can't just leave it when you get tired of it. In the case I'm talking about, though, it's too late to change anything, so I suppose it isn't really important anymore."

When he had finished eating, he went into the bedroom with Daniel. He sat on the edge of the bed as he tucked him in.

"But if you can never give up on something you started when it affects other people," Daniel continued, still thinking about what his father had said at the table, "you might have to go on all your life."

"Yes, you might," Alex agreed.

"And maybe it wouldn't do any good, anyway," Daniel went on, sitting up. "Or maybe the people don't need it."

"Daniel, what's the matter?" Alex asked, puzzled at the vehemence of his argument.

"Nothing. It's just that I worry about you," Daniel said.

"You don't have to worry about me!" Alex replied, gently stroking his son's soft, fair hair.

"Why not? You worry about me, don't you?"

"Yes, but that's because you're still too young to take care of yourself. I want to take care of you and make sure that nothing bad happens to you. Because I love you. I want you to be happy."

"Me, too," Daniel explained eagerly. "When we climb in steep places, I know you always try to stand on the downhill side of me. When I was small, it used to make me feel safe. But now I notice that sometimes you take chances to do it, and I don't like it. It makes me feel afraid for you.

And I know you do things for me even when you're tired, and that makes me feel bad. I don't want anything bad to happen to you, either, and I want you to be happy, too. Because I love you."

Alex stretched out on the living room couch and closed his eyes. Nina's face appeared on the back of his eyelids, as she had looked when she was threatening him with the knife. If he was going to see this image every time he closed his eyes, she would have her revenge after all.

Had she really wanted to kill him? Probably not badly enough to have gone through with it. A story of attempted rape wouldn't have completely explained the presence of his body in her living room. The threat effectively insured that he wouldn't accuse her of assault, but in any case, it would have given him no satisfaction to bring such a minor charge against her. She had actually killed two people, crimes for which she would never spend a single day in jail.

She thought that she had already been cruelly punished. In addition to losing her job, she had forever lost the man she loved. He would have to be satisfied with that, since the law couldn't touch her.

Nina preferred her murders to be done by someone else, while she herself stayed safely in the background. Killing by thought would suit her perfectly, but she didn't seem to have the knack. If she had, Orli would have long since disappeared.

If it was possible to kill by wishing, was it necessary to have a special talent or skill, something that Nina lacked but that Shosh perhaps had? It might require a concentration of purpose that not everyone could muster, an instant of single-minded thought focused laserlike on the target and finding it unerringly, even half a world away.

That was an interesting fancy but not relevant, since it was Nina, with her byzantine manipulations, who had caused Ilan's death. Shosh had nothing to do with it. Only—how did she know about it, in Eilat, as soon as it happened?